# BETHING'S
# FOLLY

# BETHING'S FOLLY

Barbara Metzger

WALKER AND COMPANY • NEW YORK

First published in the United States of America in 1981 by the Walker Publishing Company, Inc.

Published simultaneously in Canada by Beaverbooks, Limited, Don Mills, Ontario.

ISBN  0-8027-0677-0

**Library of Congress Cataloging in Publication Data**

Metzger, Barbara.
    Bething's folly.

    I. Title.
PS3563.E86B4   1981        813'.54        80-54483
ISBN 0-8027-0677-0

Book Design by Marjorie E. Reed

Printed in the United States of America

10 9 8 7 6 5 4 3 2

*To Mother, and Myra, with love*

# ONE

"Shut yer bloody trap! Don't yer know 'onest folks 'as got to sleep a' nights?"

This and other irate shouts from various windows was followed by the tossing of a slop jar onto the cobbled road, with the intention of hitting at least one of the two gentlemen disturbing the honest rest of London's working people. One look at the men in question would show that they neither worked for their livings nor had much dealing with those would-be sleepers who did. One of the gentlemen, the shorter of the two, was presently maintaining his balance with the aid of a street lamp, while the other wiped at a smudge on his coat of blue superfine with a lace-edged handkerchief with, it must be admitted, the concentration of one well in his cups. As he turned back to his friend, the lamp's light caught on his fair curls and handsome face, flushed now, showing him to be in his mid-twenties, well-built, and more than a little on the go. In fact, he was none too steady on his feet either.

"Come on, Ferddie. We're obviously not welcome in this neighbourhood."

"Can't think we'll be welcome in many neighbourhoods, come tomorrow," Ferddie replied, more to the lamppost than to his friend. The thought merely started him laughing so hard he lost his grip on the post and reeled off down the cobbles. The second gentleman caught up

1

with him and, putting one arm around the other's shoulder, half-led, half-supported his friend away into the darkness, their loud conversation and hoots of laughter echoing back through the empty streets.

Many a young woman in London might have hoped to be the topic of conversation between these two young Bucks, distinguished as they were by breeding, appearance and wealth—until, of course, she realised the nature of this predawn debate. For these two of London's most eligible bachelors, finest products of polite Society, were happily and loudly enumerating the perfidies of womanhood.

"Women, I tell you, Ferddie, are all Harpies. Scheming connivers, only out for what they can wring from a man."

"Just like my aunt," agreed Ferddie, Lord Ferdinand Milbrooke, that is, nephew to Lady Ashton-Milbrooke, hostess of the highest *ton*. His elaborate neckcloth was definitely askew and he paused at a stair grille, propping himself up to tug it into more comfortable looseness. The usual smile seemed to leave his face as the cloth unfolded, as he remembered his aunt's chilling demands. "Threatening to write m'mother if I missed her damned debutante ball. Serves her right that we didn't dance with that . . . that pasty-faced pack of pattern cards."

"You mean those sweet young ladies in their white lace and bows? Such innocence, with each calculating our yearly incomes to the penny. Why, it took nerves of steel just to walk the gauntlet of the dowagers' row. And if we had danced with their precious darlings, the scandal sheets would have us each engaged to one of them before dawn."

The thought served to return the humour to Ferddie's merry countenance, especially when he recalled Lady Ashton-Milbrooke's befuddled anger at their departure.

The lady had not been surprised to see her nephew at her daughter's come-out ball, of course, having laid dire threats concerning some unsavoury stories at his door. Her expression of delight at his arrival had more to do with his companion, the Marquis, Lord Alexander Carleton, only

2

son and heir to the Duke of Carlyle. Lord Carleton's appearance *had* to elevate her standing with the other hopeful mamas at the ball. Here was prestige indeed, despite Carleton's determinedly unmarried state and somewhat unsteady behaviour. In a less exalted noble, his erratic associations with opera-dancers, elegant Frenchwomen and certain dashing widows would have been shameful, but Lord Carleton's charm, and his family's social standing, were such that he was always forgiven and much sought after. He did not go often into Society, and was generally known to disdain any activity which smacked of the Marriage Mart. In fact, Ferddie and Carleton, together with some of their sporting or Corinthian circle, had even founded a bachelors' club, with wagers and forfeits. Most knew they would have to forego the pleasures of their carefree bachelorhoods some day, either to carry on their lines and guarantee succession to their titles, as in Carleton's case, or simply to please their families, as in Ferddie's, or to repair financial difficulties, as was the situation with many of their friends. In the meantime, none of this group eschewed female company entirely, vowing that one needn't own the vineyard in order to enjoy the wine. Enjoy it they did, especially Carleton, with his wealth, his charm and his handsome blond looks, thus far avoiding parson's mousetrap.

Whatever the cause, and no matter how plain the daughter, hope was eternal in a mama's breast, and Lady Ashton-Milbrooke was hoping Carleton's time had come. It was with him in mind, of course, that she had insisted on her nephew's appearance; for though Ferddie was himself eligible and pleasing and well set-up, with a generous income to boot, his most promising attribute was Carleton at his side.

With all of these hopeful strategies wafting ahead of her, Lady Ashton-Milbrooke had gracefully crossed the dance floor to greet the arrival of the gentlemen long after the dancing had begun, wondering upon which of the young ladies, beside her own Clarice, of course, she should bestow them. As surely as she knew Ferddie would appear, she was guaranteed having him for at least two so-called duty dances, and his friend as well. She was justifiably beaming at matrons to either side as her nephew made his bow. She had no more turned to look for her daughter than my Lord Carleton firmly grasped her arm and swirled her, the hostess, long past this sort of thing, out to the floor in the middle of a dance. She was swooped and twirled with a masterful grace she was quite unused to and found herself instantly out of breath. She had one flustered glimpse of Ferddie, dancing with Clarice, before the music ended.

"One's duties as a guest should always be such a pleasure, ma'am," Carleton said, raising her hand to be kissed, causing the dizzy lady to look for the irony; all she saw was a lopsided grin showing a dimple, no less.

Graceless scamp, she thought, before recalling herself. But Carleton was already taking Clarice's hand for the next country dance. Quite properly, too, the mother felt, enchanted in spite of her own better judgement. The figures of the dance made conversation difficult; Miss Clarice's shyness at being confronted with her first genuine Rake made it almost impossible. Perhaps it was her silence, or some other deviltry, which prompted the Marquis to pluck a flower from an urn as he led the young lady back to her mother at the end of the dance. He solemnly tucked it in the curls of her hair and, bending, whispered so only she could hear: "Just wait, darling, till you are an elegant married lady. *Then* we'll have a lot to say to each other."

Bowing once more to Lady Ashton-Milbrooke, Carleton took Ferddie's arm and, turning, the two most prized matrimonial catches of that London Season departed, downing a glass of champagne each from a tray by the door. They left behind them a furiously blushing young lady and a just furious older one. Never had Lady Ashton-Milbrooke seen social duties performed with such elegance, granted, but neither with such expediency! The memory of being

4

glided around like a young girl clashed with the necessity of finding partners for a whole clutch of giggling be-ribboned misses. Ferddie Milbrooke's mother would certainly be informed of his all-too-brief appearance. There would even be slurs on Carleton's character—whatever had he said to poor Clarice, who would now be tongue-tied for the rest of the evening?—and a warning that soon no respectable parents would permit even Ferddie to approach their daughters, if he persisted in such fast company.

The two friends, many hours later, were still chuckling over Lady Ashton-Milbrooke's consternation.

"Did you see Aunt's face after your dance with her? It was as purple as her turban!"

"But did you see all those debutantes she had lined up for us? Like so many fancy dolls in a shop window, and with about as much to say," now commented that same fast company, fumbling with his buttons after relieving himself behind a drayer's cart.

"Well, your little thrush at the dance hall didn't have much conversation either." Ferddie laughed at the memory, which again threw his balance off, causing him to clutch at Carleton's arm, not aiding that gentleman's difficulties. "But at least she was dressed better than my cousin."

"Only because she was dressed less!"

"Well, what was her name, anyway?"

"Your cousin?" asked Carleton, finally taking the other's arm and continuing on the way.

"No, of course not. She's Lucinda. No, Lucinda is the one that got married last year. This one must be Clarice. Yes, I think that's it. But what was the name of the girl at Covent Gardens?"

"Damned if I know," was the reply.

Upon leaving Lady Ashton-Milbrooke quaking behind them, the two noblemen had repaired to the dance hall. There was talk in the clubs of a new girl singing there, and bets were being recorded at White's on which of the young bucks would receive her favours. Odds of her remaining independent, without a protector, past one week's time were very low. Carleton and Ferddie had seen enough in the scanty costume during the show to pass backstage to the dressing rooms for an introduction and a closer look shortly before the closing curtains. There had been a whole queue of stage-door Johnnies hanging about, laughing and joking, until they saw Carleton.

"Damn, Carleton," called Lord Rutley, a friend and member of the bachelor club. "Did you come just to ruin all our chances?"

"What, did you think you had any? I heard she was holding out for higher stakes." And the gentlemen had all laughed some more, many of them ruefully acknowledging the truth of this, and sheepishly counting themselves out of the running. Some of the others, well aware of Carleton's reputation—both of his appeal to women and his temper— also left, feeling it was not worth the trouble when there were so many other pretty, less demanding, already soiled doves to entertain them. Granted, Carleton no longer issued challenges over the merest fancied insult, nor instigated brawls, as in his schoolboy days; but he was still no one the younger men chose to cross, especially with Ferddie along to back him up, so they departed. This left only Lord Cleighchester, a paunchy, middle-aged baronet. When a query into the health of his good wife and children only served to redden the man's face somewhat, it was followed by curiosity as to the ages of the happy progeny. Lord Cleighchester was finally discomfited by the pointed observance that the lady in question was some five years younger than Cleighchester's own daughter, and wasn't it strange how some girls could count on their fathers to protect them and others were at the mercy of the streets. Mumbling about a prior engagement, the baronet hurried off, leaving the two friends alone and laughing when the dressing-room door was opened.

"See how easy success can be?" Carleton asked Ferddie.

The manager, quite readily recognising Milbrooke and Carleton, stepped aside to let them enter, calculating his share if an arrangement should be made with Milbrooke. Regrettably, Carleton was known to maintain a mistress in Bank Street in elegant style, unless, of course, he had tired of the lady and was looking for her successor. The manager's hopes rose, for Carleton was the wealthier of the two. He was sure the new girl would prefer the strikingly handsome Marquis over the pleasant-looking Milbrooke, but much her opinion would matter.

The actress herself smiled prettily up at the two callers and invited them to be seated, then offered them brandy from a decanter. As she poured, her eyes flickered from Carleton's elegantly embroidered waistcoat to Milbrooke's single gold fob, noting Carleton's diamond stickpin, Milbrooke's ruby signet. Carleton's angel blue eyes made her catch her breath, but Milbrooke's friendly smile warmed her nervousness. Her smile widened in return, and her eyelashes fluttered as the lady finished her inspection and passed the drinks, well aware that she in turn was on review. She thrust her shoulders back and tossed her silvery curls, seeing her dreams come true right before her eyes. All difficulties with the manager would be resolved, and uncertainties about her future. She had been right to leave the small farming town and find her fortune here, with either of these fine gentlemen—the cool, handsome one with all his fine clothes and taut muscles, or the easier, plainer, but somehow cozier one. She closed her eyes to picture herself wearing the cameo brooch in the Bond Street window, coming back to the theatre in a closed carriage to flaunt her good fortune at the other girls. All this took place in minutes, during which not a word was said.

Ferddie, looking a little uncertainly at his friend, tried to start a conversation. "That was a very, um, lovely performance you gave tonight. The audience enjoyed it."

The girl simpered in acknowledgement and sipped at her drink, congratulating herself on how well things were going. She repeated to herself the manager's orders: "Look pretty and keep yer trap shut." These fine gentlemen would never talk to a lady like that, she didn't doubt. She turned to Carleton, casting her eyes down in expectation of *his* compliment, thus permitting Milbrooke to view her delightful profile. This meant, of course, that she could not see the looks which passed between the two men. She only looked up in time to see both callers rising and hear Carleton say, "Good evening, madam. It has been a pleasure to converse with you. I am certain you will be a great success at your chosen career." And both opportunities withdrew from her dressing room and daydreams, leaving the poor girl almost swooning—no act this time— then a lot nearer to a tantrum when she realised that all of her other admirers had deserted her.

What sounded like a perfume bottle crashed into the door behind the departing guests, followed perhaps by a rouge pot or a mirror before they were out of hearing, laughingly enjoining a waitress to find them a table and bring them a bottle to celebrate yet another escape.

Somewhere partly through the second bottle after that one the friends decided to go separate ways, Carleton to visit his Yvette on Bank Street, Milbrooke to join a game of faro at one of the clubs. It was with considerable surprise, therefore, that Ferddie saw his companion's athletic form in the doorway of White's less than an hour later.

"Never say the lady threw you out, Carleton?" he teased.

"Women, I tell you, are not to be trusted! Every last one will take all you have to give and what do you get in return? Lies, and tears, and... and inferior brandy."

"You mean you left the most desirable creature in all of England because the wine was no good?"

"No, damn it, I left because someone else was drinking my stock."

"Ah, entertaining callers, was she?"

"Just some old friends from France, who dropped by unexpectedly this afternoon, she said. I would have believed her, too, if not for the emeralds. There she was, as exquisite as ever, with that black hair tumbling over her shoulders and skin so white, and those big green eyes you could drown in. A natural for emeralds, right?"

Ferddie just nodded dreamily, lost in the vision in his mind.

"I bought her a gorgeous set a while ago, choker and bracelet; no one can say I denied her anything. But she was wearing diamonds. When I asked her to change, do you know what she said?"

"They didn't match her gown?" Ferddie guessed.

"She wasn't wearing any gown, you clunch. No, she said they were being cleaned. Being copied in paste, I'd say, if not sold already. Oh, she tried to cloud the issue, crying that I didn't trust her when she tried *so* hard to please me. I started to look around though. One or two of the miniatures were missing, and a few odds and ends I recalled giving her. Funny what a fellow starts to notice once he opens his eyes. Anyway, she started to enact a whole Cheltenham tragedy about this fellow countryman in desperate need. Lost everything in the Terror, of course, has nothing to live on ... you know the story. She was pawning my gifts for money to give to him. All innocent, of course."

"Did you believe her?"

"Well, she was ready to be very persuasive. The butler was a little more forthright. After all, I do pay his salary. It seems Madame's caller usually arrived after the butler was dismissed, long after I had left, surely not the case of an old friend asking for help."

"Did the chap give you any idea of the man's identity?"

"Not definitely, but with a little golden reminder he

was able to recall a certain French count. I've heard he's on the lookout for an heiress, hanging around the gaming tables in the meantime. I'm sure you've seen him around. The dice are always against him. It would seem he has changed his luck, or his game, the dog."

"Will you call him out?"

"What for? Hunting on my preserves? No, I've no proof. Besides, no wench is worth it. I've done with Yvette. They can *both* starve for all I care."

"So which rankles most, the idea of Yvette sharing her, um, favours, or sharing your money?"

"Actually, what galls me the worst is the idea of that damned Frenchman drinking the last of my finest French brandy. Women, I tell you, Ferddie, are all Harpies."

So it was that the two gentlemen found themselves in the dark streets, having visited several more of their clubs to discuss the cunning strengths of the weaker sex, be they of the *haute-monde*, the *demi-monde*, or the baser haunts of the nobility.

Carleton congratulated himself on his freedom, and Milbrooke happily anticipated the morning's gossip. Pleased with their night's activity and each other's company, they finally reached Milbrooke's front door.

# TWO

"Well, here you are, Ferddie," said Carleton outside the door to Milbrooke's lodgings. "What are your plans for the morning? Will you attend the mill at Stuart's?"

"Um, what morning is that? Tuesday? Yes, I think so. Will you drive?" And the two continued walking a half-block farther to Carleton's townhouse, a handsome grey stone building. They paused outside the ironwork gates as Carleton invited his friend in for a parting drink. Ferddie declined, unsteadily pointing to the first lightening of the dawn, wondering how many hours away was the morning's activity. So they walked back to Milbrooke's, discussing the odds set for the day's match and the company they could look forward to meeting. At last they parted and Carleton walked home alone, humming none too softly but carefully watching his footsteps so they stayed in a line.

He hesitated when he reached the gates again, looking up with a fond, pleased smile at the lights left burning for him. The house came nowhere near the magnificence of his family's London home, Carlyle House in Berkeley Square, nor the newer elegance of Yvette's, but here was the Marquis's private refuge. It was filled with his books, the smell of his tobacco, his dogs and, often as not, his cronies. There was nothing spindly or fragile in it, only good, sturdy stuff a man could be comfortable with. The house was staffed with a butler and a cook-housekeeper who had

11

followed him from his father's estates, leaving positions as under-servants to run a household of their own for the young master when he was just out of school. His valet had been born on the estate and had come to Carleton when the Marquis was only sixteen, a level-headed gentleman's gentleman who hoped to have a restraining influence on the young lord. Other household help was hired when there was need, such as entertaining or major housecleaning, and the few cleaning girls who came in by day were never allowed to intrude on Carleton's privacy—whether through the offices of Mrs. Henrys, his housekeeper, or their own mamas, he never knew. His secretary, a distant younger relative of his father, the Duke, also came in by day, to go over accounts, engagements and correspondence. Carleton, in fact, concerned himself not a bit with the daily workings of his household, only knowing himself comfortable, well-fed and vaguely grateful to be excused from such considerations as servants, budgets and menus.

It was only moments such as these, his head already beginning to ache, his clothes a little disordered, that he wished to be surrounded only by strangers or, better yet, ignored, instead of seeing the concern and disapproval on the faces of old family retainers.

Ah, well, he thought, he was home before dawn—just— and no one was expected to wait up for him. Nevertheless, he straightened his broad shoulders, put his head to one side and whistled the racy tune making the rounds of the clubs. Feigning jauntiness he was far from feeling, he entered his own gates.

The moment the gates swung to, the front door was opened and light flooded the walk. Henrys was standing just inside, not showing any signs of anxiety or reproof, merely behaving as though butlers always welcomed their masters home at five in the morning. Carleton looked around enquiringly but nothing showed out of the ordinary. Henrys took his coat and asked, as he always did, if his lordship had had a pleasant evening and if there was anything he might wish. Then and only then, custom fulfilled, he coughed gently and mentioned that a letter had been delivered somewhat earlier in the evening.

"A letter, Henrys? Don't tell me you waited up to give me a letter! No, not now. Give it to Mr. Sebastian in the morning, or burn it, for all I care!"

Henrys cleared his throat again. "Yes, my Lord, but I did feel you might wish to see it, sir. It's from the Hall." And he held out a thick page sealed in blue with the ducal crest.

"From the Duke? Why didn't you say so, man?" exclaimed Carleton, ripping open the page. All signs of weariness were suddenly gone, all the boyish merriment and even the flush of indulgence. He read through the short note and then absently folded it over again.

"I have been requested to attend his Grace at my earliest convenience, which could only mean something urgent, or he would have put it in the note. What time did this arrive? Why wasn't I sent for?"

"It arrived about eleven, my Lord, and I did consider it somewhat out of the ordinary, a messenger arriving like that. But the boy did not know of any, um, misfortune at the Hall. I called for Jeremy at the stables and sent him round to Lady Ashton-Milbrooke's rout, sir, but you had left somewhat, um, early, he was told." Henrys was choosing his words with care, being obviously more informed than his master knew or desired. "I sent him to Bank Street then, but he was, um, not admitted?" The question here was rather hopefully put. When no information was forthcoming, Henrys continued: "Finally Jeremy went round to Watiers, but you'd not been there, and White's, but you had already left. Then we, Mrs. Henrys and I, sir, felt Jeremy could perhaps be needed here, when you returned. He's waiting for your orders at the stable."

"Right, Henrys. You'll have to go tell him to fetch my horse round in about twenty minutes while I change. Also, he'll follow with the chaise as soon as Ainsley packs my bags. And make sure the boy from Carlyle is ready to go with them unless he has business in town. Yes, and I'll need something to eat along the way. Do you think you could raid Mrs. Henrys's pantry for me?"

"Oh, there is no need, sir. She has a breakfast packed for you, and Ainsley is waiting upstairs with your riding clothes ready. Your valise is already in the chaise. And Mrs. Henrys can have tea laid out for you in just a moment, when you've done changing."

Carleton was momentarily stunned at the thoroughness of his employees. If they'd had to drag him unconscious from some gaming hell and tie him to the back of his horse, he was sure they would do it, yes, and see he was shaved and sober before greeting his father, to boot! He could only mutter words about his profound appreciation before bounding up the stairs. Ainsley was waiting for him as promised, ready with a hot basin of water to wash in, fresh clothes and shining riding boots. His greatcoat was laid out on the bed in case of an early morning chill, next to a saddle pack containing merely Carleton's shaving equipment and a clean shirt. He had duplicates of everything he'd need at Carlyle Hall and could easily make do until his valet arrived.

"I expect to be at Carlyle by midafternoon, Ainsley. I'll only stop to change horses once, if I can manage. Do you get there as quickly as possible. I'll look for you towards midnight."

Ainsley agreed, silently dreading the ride with only the groom at the ribbons. It would only be the care Jeremy took of his master's horseflesh that would save Ainsley's skin. He did not mention his own worries, of course, noting the grave concern on Lord Carleton's face as he hurriedly fitted him into his riding jacket and pulled on his boots. He could not help a smidgeon of satisfaction, thinking how the young master would do Ainsley proud in front of Greaves, the Duke's arrogant man. Thoughts of the Duke and his uncertain health returned to mind the gravity of the moment; Ainsley quickly draped the caped greatcoat over Carleton's wide shoulders.

Carleton strode down the stairs for a quick drink of something hot, some toast and jam, and a few final instructions to Henrys about sending a note round to Milbrooke and having Sebastian take care of other commitments.

In precisely twenty-two minutes from his entry to the house, horses were heard at the gates. Carleton grabbed the appreciation once more and was off, almost running down one of the housemaids coming for her morning's work. She jumped aside and clicked her tongue at the goings-on of the nobility. Almost every day she had to tiptoe round at her chores while the master slept; here it was, barely six o'clock, and he was careening around the town like he had an honest job to get to. Oh, well, at least now she might hum to make the morning go faster.

# THREE

Noontime found Lord Carleton at a staging house, downing a tankard of ale while horses were brought around for his inspection. He certainly looked different from the polished London Dandy of the dawn, with his face covered with dust and his clothes and boots spattered with mud and grime. The grim lines around his mouth replacing the ready smile attested to the seriousness of his ride. He'd spent the last hours encouraging his tired mount and agonising over what amounted to a midnight summons to Carlyle Hall. "At his earliest convenience," indeed! With no hint as to the reason for the message, only the worst could be expected. It must be his father's health, he supposed, for the old Duke had had warnings of heart ailment in the past. Let him only be in time, he thought now, impatiently smacking his riding crop against his topboots as another sway-backed old hay-burner was led out of the stables. The Duchess, he recalled, had been in perfect glowing health just last month when he'd attended her at her visit to London for a rare two-day shopping excursion. The Duke had not accompanied her, claiming business on the estate, which now seemed suspect. But no, his lady mother had seemed untroubled, and surely any concern felt through her great love of the Duke must have been apparent.

Carleton's mouth relaxed as he recalled the two days he had escorted the Duchess, the sweetest, most feminine woman of his acquaintance. He remembered the pride he had felt at having such a lady on his arm at the opera's doors. Some twenty years younger than the Duke, the Duchess was still a great beauty, but now with the assurance and calm poise which made her a great lady. Carleton had even to discourage a few middle-aged courtiers from making advances. The box had been full of them at intermission. The Duchess had laughed her chiming enjoyment and said what fun it would give the Duke to hear of her success.

The Duke, Carleton thought, and the urgent need to get home swelled up again. He selected the only sound-looking horse in the lot, a wide-chested beast. He paid his shot while vowing never to patronize this particular hostelry again, and was off once the mount was saddled, scattering pebbles and stable help both.

The Duke of Carlyle was indeed in his bed that morning, a massive four-poster hung with antique draperies. The tapestries were pulled back now, and the Duke was fretfully surrounded by his doctor, his man of business and the curate. His valet stood by the window, holding the curtains aside to watch for the Marquis's arrival. He heard a muttered "Damn" from his Grace and anxiously turned to catch the pained expression on the Duke's face as he tossed his cards down on the deal table pulled next to his bed.

"I've no patience for whist today, gentlemen, my apologies. In truth, I dislike being around the house all day, to say nothing of wearing nightclothes when I should be out." And he plucked at the white gown. "But what must be must be. Greaves, keep an eye to that window. It's early yet, but he might arrive sooner than expected."

"Only if the Marquis was at home, your Grace," soothed Mr. Campion, the Duke's old friend and solicitor, called down from London to be accomplice, not altogether unwilling, in the Duke's current scheme to get his son settled in life. "No, Lord Alexander would have had to leave London at eleven last night to arrive at the Hall soon."

"Which he damn well did not," growled the Duke. "From what I hear and what the Duchess gathered, the damn cub never sleeps at home. He is leading a round of... of dissolution. And don't look at me like that, Reverend. I may have been a wild youth, yes, and married late in life like the Carletons always have, but at least I had brothers behind me to insure the succession. Alexander has no one, so *must* do his duty—and soon, too. I'll not have my brother Jack's damn progeny sleeping in my bed!"

Anger at the thought—though he would be long dead before it happened—mingled with regret in the Duke's mind. There had been other children, a boy first, dark like himself but so sickly the second winter was too much for him. Then Alexander, with his mother's blond looks and cherubic beauty, a good, sturdy lad. Then two infants dead at birth, a girl and another boy. After that the Duke had refused to allow his wife another pregnancy. Even the offspring of Jack and the ninnyhammer he had married taking his—and Alexander's—place was preferable to endangering his lady-wife. No, she was more precious than even that consideration. But now Alexander, coddled and spoiled and loved beyond the share of any four children, must live up to the obligations of his centuries-old name. And soon, while the Duke could enjoy his grandchildren and the peace of knowing Alexander comfortably settled at last. Yes, this had to succeed.

"What time is it, Campion?" he asked irritably.

"Almost noon, your Grace."

"How about a small wager?" asked the doctor, also invited just for the show and enjoying himself immensely on the good food and good company. "I say he gets here within the hour, riding. Or do you think he'll drive?"

"No, I'm sure he will ride. You're on! I say he would not receive the message till morning, and, leaving immediately, one change of horse, riding like the devil, he should be here by five."

"I had to put up overnight on my way down," considered the solicitor. "That was in your Grace's chaise, of course, but the roads were in deplorable conditions, what with the rain. Supposing you are correct and Lord Alexander leaves London at six or seven, for you must know his habits best, I still say it must take twelve hours. Seven this evening is my bet."

"The boy can do it in ten," the Duke stated, positively and proudly. "I was known to make good time myself once. He'll not stick to the roads, either. I'll be bound he comes cross-country and shaves time that way." The Duke spoke with assurance. He knew what was due him as the head of the family, but he also knew what would be freely given, out of love and concern. In fact, he was counting on it.

The curate now entered the conversation for the first time. He was not averse to a game of whist and certainly not shocked at the suggestion of a wager. He had readily acquiesced to the Duke's deception and was, in fact, pleased to be invited to join the company. Furthermore, the Duke had always been generous to the parish and would be, presumably, more so in the future. All material considerations aside, however, the curate's sympathies were always with the underdog and now his sensibilities were bothered. "Your Grace, don't you think it somewhat hard on the boy, asking him to travel all day, with no sleep, under uncomfortable and perhaps dangerous conditions, while suffering grave concerns over your Grace's health?"

"Nonsense. All that will merely lower his defenses! Do you think we could pull this off if the boy was rested and at ease to think about it? No, the timing and worry are a necessary part of the plan." The Duke chuckled. "And I need all the advantages I can gather. So come, Reverend, your sympathies are becoming but wasted here. What is your wager?"

The reverend politely and politically selected a time much later than the Duke's guess, which he considered accurate, ready to compliment the Duke on the proof of his son's devotion when the Marquis arrived earlier. The curate was often, in this company, weighing wisdom against scruples, with the truth bending somewhat for convenience. He said a silent prayer for forgiveness while the wager was modestly fixed, Greaves holding the money.

Next under consideration was how quickly a wedding could decently be staged without giving gossip a breeding ground once the Marquis had selected a bride. Which of course led to consideration of the local young ladies of standing, if no bride was forthcoming from London, which the Duke thought improbable.

"No, if he was paying court to any of the debutantes we would have heard of it by now. These things get talked about, you know. I'd be surprised if he even *knew* any suitable females!" the Duke said with a scowl. Then not wishing to belabour the issue, he invited his guests to go downstairs to partake of what he hoped would be a satisfactory luncheon. "I wish I could join you, but mustn't take the risk. Greaves, see the gentlemen out, then find me a tray or something. Mr. Campion, please make a toast to our success . . . and, Reverend, do say a prayer."

When his guests had departed, the Duke did in fact get under the covers and lean back against his pillows. He closed his eyes and his face did look weary, with deep lines etched under the thick hair, still dark but with the temples almost white. Yes, he was getting old, he admitted to himself. It would be well to get this settled. Then one side of his mouth twitched upward in anticipation and the eyes snapped open, glittering, giving him a decidedly youthful, mischievous look—a look, in fact, which was very familiar to his son's associates.

There was a soft knock on the door and the Duchess entered, an exquisite portrait of stately blonde beauty with a bouquet of miniature roses in a crystal vase. When she caught the expression on the Duke's face, her smile of welcome faded. The Duchess's eyebrows came together and her lower lip was fixed with determination, but she held her peace while a series of footmen covered the deal table with white linen and Sèvres china for two. The Duchess set the vase in the center of the table, putting it down with an audible *thud*.

"I have decided to join you for luncheon, if I may, your Grace," were the Duchess's polite words, "though I was sorely tempted to have Greaves bring you some thin gruel, suitable for one in your 'condition.'" Nothing but pleasantries were exchanged while the footmen served from silver-covered dishes, then withdrew. The Duke poured himself another glass of wine and looked at his wife closely.

"All right, my dear, what is it that has you burning with indignation? Come on, Claire, out with it so I may enjoy my wine. You are not going soft on me, are you? You know we decided it was time we took a hand in the matter."

"No, sir. *You* decided. But, yes, I was willing to let you play this cruel hoax on poor Alexander, but... but you need not enjoy it so much! That is what galls me. He must be worrying himself sick, and you lay there reveling in your schemes, taking pleasure in tricking him and... and smirking!"

The Duke laughed outright. "Yes, Claire, I am enjoying myself hugely, and I am sorry you're disturbed by it. But remember how much worry the dratted cub has caused us? Haven't you been in a turmoil over his reckless ways, afraid he would make himself thoroughly unacceptable to any decent family, or worse? I am only paying him back a little—it's only for a day or two—and you'll see, it will be worth it."

"You're sure it will work?" asked the Duchess, all resentment spent the moment it was mentioned, now only concern left to crease her brow.

"It worked on me, didn't it? Why, my father must have lived thirty years after his 'deathbed' scene. If it hadn't been for the promise he tore out of me then, I am sure I would never have married. No"—the look on his wife's face caused him to hurry on—"I have never regretted it for one instant, my dear. Never. I loved you the moment I set eyes on you; but I never would have been looking, except for such a prank."

"But what if he marries the wrong woman just to please you? What if he selects someone he cannot grow to love and must live with her the rest of his life, never knowing the happiness we have found?"

The Duke took her hand across the table and held it tightly in both of his. "Claire, my beautiful, precious duchess, he will not—he cannot—choose the wrong woman. He is my son."

# FOUR

At precisely ten minutes to five hooves sounded in the long ride leading up to Carlyle Hall and a groom sprang from the stables. A horse came to view through the trees, white with lather, laboring but still game. The rider jumped off when he neared the groom, not bothering to hand the reins over, just bounding up the wide steps to the double doors. The horse merely lowered its head; Carleton called back over his shoulder: "See you cool him off well and bed him down. He's done a good job." Then he pulled open the doors, not waiting for the butler or footmen, who were hurrying at the sound of visitors. He grasped the butler by his shoulders.

"My father?"

"His Grace is upstairs resting, Lord Alexander. Lady Claire is in her rooms. Mr. Campion, the doctor and Reverend Albright are in the blue parlour. Shall I—"

But Carleton was past him, down the hall, throwing his wet, muddy coat over a gilded chair. He glanced into the door on his right where the three men were speaking in subdued voices over glasses of port, but he did not greet them. He looked up at the double-arched staircase, then bounded up the nearest flight. Without pausing to knock, he burst in to the Duke's bedroom at the head of the stairs but came to a halt as he took a step into the darkened room. The curtains were drawn and only a single candelabrum cast faint light on the Duke in his bed across the vast room.

From this distance the Duke seemed small in his enormous bed, and almost colourless against the white of his pillows and nightclothes, the dark of his hair the only accent.

How pale he looks, thought Carleton, how vulnerable. He had never considered his father like this, old, weak, without the vital strength the Duke had always seemed to personify.

He walked over to the bed as softly as he could in topboots, leaving a trail of caked mud on the hand-tied carpet, and silently drew a chair up to the bedstead. He sat there, staring at his father for what seemed an age. At last the old man's eyes slowly opened part way, closed, then widened again in surprised recognition.

"Alexander? Is it you, son?" The voice was only a whisper.

"Yes, your Grace. I am here. I came as soon as I got your message. How do you, sir?"

"Ah, Alexander. The doctor says I . . . I don't know how long I . . ."

"Don't speak, Father. All will be well. You'll see. You'll have a good rest, that's all. You've most likely been working too hard, taking too much on. Those doctors don't know everything; you've said it often enough yourself."

"But so many things . . . the crops . . ."

"No, Father. You have a bailiff for that. I'll speak to Mr. Caulfield myself. I can manage, really I can. But you must rest." Carleton made as if to rise, but the Duke lifted one hand from the bed. The hand fell back, as if the effort was too much.

"No, Alex, I have to talk . . . something important . . ."

Carleton settled himself again, leaning closer to make it easier for the Duke to be heard. "Anything, Father, anything."

The old Duke sighed and looked up at his son through eyes half-closed as though in weariness. "Alex," he said, then paused to catch his breath. "Alex, I cannot find peace; I cannot rest easy for worrying. What will happen to all this?" The same tired hand made a circle over the counter-

26

pane. "I had wanted to know your sons, to see them grow, to teach them to love this place as I do, as I thought you did."

"Of course I do, your Grace, but what—"

"Please, Alex, while there is still time . . . please promise me you will marry soon, and let an old man die happy."

"Do not speak like that, Father! Of course I promise. But I—"

"Soon, Alexander? Within months, while I still have strength to welcome your bride?"

Carleton looked down at the man laid in his bed, the hand already too weak to grip his firmly, and gave his solemn oath.

"Ah, Alexander," and the voice was miraculously stronger, "now I can rest." The Duke's eyes were drifting shut but he opened them a last time and smiled faintly at his son. "Go to your mother now, Alexander. She will be needing you." His nose wrinkled slightly. "But, Alex, do change your clothes first."

It was a subdued Lord Carleton who went down the hall to his own rooms. He silently nodded to Greaves, who just as silently helped him off with his boots. A footman brought hot water to fill a tub, but not a word was spoken beyond "thank you" and "that will be all."

Carleton dressed himself in a coat of blue superfine, then slowly and methodically tied his neckcloth in front of the mirror. He combed his blond curls through with his fingers, still staring at the image, almost looking for an answer there to some deep, unspoken question. At last he walked past his father's door to his mother's suite and tapped softly at the door.

The Duchess herself opened the door and stood still a moment, seeing the dark circles under Carleton's eyes, the weary look to his mouth, the deep lines at his forehead, the droop to his shoulders.

"Oh, Alex," she cried, and stepped forward to hold him in her arms as she would a child, this boy—man now—who stood so tall.

Misreading her emotion as grief, Carleton awkwardly tried to comfort her. He held her close, gently patting her back as she rested her cheek on his shoulder, her golden head incidentally creasing his fresh neckcloth. "There, my Lady, all will be well. Come, sit by me." And he led her to a window seat where velvet hangings made a frame for her lavender gown. Two pairs of blue eyes exchanged worried looks until the Duchess had to lower hers. Carleton took her hands and squared his broad shoulders.

"Mother, I"—he cleared his throat—"I need your help. I . . . I have made a promise."

# FIVE

A ball was planned at Carlyle Hall for a short few weeks later, a ball of such grandeur its like had not been seen in the county in recent memory. The dance was ostensibly the Duke's gift to his niece Margaret, Jack's daughter, to announce her engagement to Captain Mark Hendricks, which explained all the scarlet regimentals seemingly billeted at Carle Manor, Margaret's home. Carlyle Hall itself would host many of London's finest families, all manner of distant relations and a near-score of Carleton's own friends. The young men were invited for a week's hunting, and to sustain Carleton, though only Ferddie Milbrooke knew the desperateness of the case.

Not everyone could accept the Duchess's kind invitation, of course, owing to the haste of preparation and previous engagements—the Prince of Wales, for one, was abroad but sent his regrets. It must be noted that among the refusals, not a single one was from a household with an eligible daughter.

Margaret's engagement might serve for propriety, but rumours were as thick as starlings on the lawn. For the local gentry there were too many people—and servants—who knew otherwise. Every housemaid and groom with a connection to the Hall was suddenly known by name. The details were mere speculation, but the Duke's intentions were not. As for Town, there were just too many young women invited for coincidence. Even the Duchess could not claim kinship with so many families. Perhaps, gossip went, the Marquis was in difficulties with some outraged husband and this was the solution. The dowagers gloated— it was about time the impudent cub was leg-shackled— while betting at White's filled an entire page: Would the Duke pull it off? How soon? What were the chances of the Season's Beauties? Carleton wisely remained at the Hall in the country.

The Marquis had no need to seek an heiress, which brought joy to the hearts of mamas whose daughters were more blessed with beauty than material endowment. Those of more generous means spent a deal of it improving the debutante's physical assets. Such a flurry of activity kept every seamstress between London and Carlyle Hall burning candles late into the nights. The country misses, especially, did not want to be eclipsed by their London cousins and had their ball gowns cut a little lower, their stays pulled a little tighter, their hair piled a little higher. There was a rush at the dancing instructors of the vicinity also, for the waltz would be performed. Some of the local mothers had never seen the waltz danced and only knew it by reputation. They worried lest their daughters be considered fast for dancing, or dowdy for sitting it out. Much tea was consumed over deliberation of this question, which was finally settled with the argument that, after all, if the Duchess of Carlyle permitted it in her home, the waltz must be unexceptionable. All around the countryside and among those soon to be assembling at the Hall, delicious anticipation was another house guest.

At the Hall itself there was much less time for deliberation. Extra staff was hired from the village and even borrowed from Carle Manor. Not merely extra bedrooms but entire unused wings of the ancient rambling castle were opened to house the great numbers of guests. Dinner for the ball must be planned and preparations started, and meals and entertainment for the weekend house guests.

The gardens had to provide decoration for the immense ballroom, each guest's bedchamber, and the rest of the house—without looking bare to anyone out for a stroll. The hothouses had to provide corsages for all the lady guests, and out-of-season fruit. The silver had to be polished, the linen must be aired, the champagne ordered. All of these duties naturally fell to the capable hands of Lady Claire, Duchess of Carlyle, to organize, besides the complicated guest lists themselves. That lady glided as smoothly and gracefully through all the details as the black swans glided on the Hall's twin lakes. Carlyle Hall was always well run, of course, but the Duchess won even more admiration for her sweet, even nature, especially in a decidedly trying situation. For if all the preparations for the ball itself were well in hand, the tempers of the Carlyle menfolk, father and son, were definitely strained.

The Duke, whose nature had never been exactly even, was chafing under the enforced seclusion in his upstairs chambers "for his health's sake." An extremely active man, used to overseeing every detail of his vast holding himself, he was furious at having to wait for his bailiff's reports. When it was decided to open unused portions of the cavernous stables to house the horses of the weekend guests, the Duke ached to supervise, to see it was done well. Instead, Lord Alexander went to see what repairs were necessary, what farm hands must be called in to help, what other out-buildings could serve to store equipment moved from unused stalls. Carleton worked right alongside the men, delighted to have an occupation outside the furious activity in the house. His absence only aggravated the Duke's boredom and irritation, as now no one had time for a chess game or a round of piquet, except for the doctor's *pro forma* visits every other day. When the Duke grumbled to his wife in the rare moments she had to spend with him, she merely smiled and sweetly reminded his Grace that he had no one but himself to blame. At last he declared himself well enough to dress and go down to meals, but his son's solicitude grated on his nerves—"No, I do *not* need your arm down the stairs. No, I do *not* require a tonic"—and the haunted look in Lord Alexander's eyes did not aid his digestion, or disposition.

Lord Carleton himself, the unwilling object of all this activity, had unfortunately inherited a great deal of his father's temper. He refused to think a ball at Carlyle was proper now with his father's health so precarious, and grew more vehement about it the closer the date came.

"But, Alexander," his mother would try to reason, "the invitations have all been sent."

"Well, call them back. His Grace should have quiet in the house, to rest, not this . . . this pandemonium. We could have a small dinner in a few months, invite some of the local families when the Duke is more the thing. Or I could just—"

"No, dear, the Duke wishes to have the ball here, now. He believes it will cheer him to have the house filled with all his friends and so many young people. And I think so, too. Of course he must have his rest—he only comes down for his meals—and see how much stronger he is getting already?"

Alexander merely glowered. His father was obviously growing more crotchety, if nothing else.

The situation was becoming more awkward daily, the Duke prowling around, interfering with the busy household servants, and Carleton threatening to return to London, until his friends started to arrive at last. He threw himself into their entertainment—hunting and riding all day, his father's best brandies half the night—as though this was his last week of pleasure. The Duke, finally free of his son's scrutiny, could go for short rides around the estate, praising the stable crews, encouraging the gardeners, making suggestions to his bailiff. When Carleton returned with his friends for meals, he could not help but note the healthy colouring returning daily to his father's complexion, his better frame of mind. Carleton shook his head ruefully as he stared at his wine glass; at least some good was coming from this wretched ball.

Carlyle Hall was magnificent. Lights gleamed in all the hundreds of windows, the silver birch trees along the drive were hung with lanterns and to the rear fairy lights twinkled over the causeway between the twin lakes. The carriages were lined up for miles, it seemed, but they discharged passengers four at a time at the wide marble steps. Smiling blue-liveried attendants were everywhere. Not one carriage door had to wait to be opened, not one lady had to pause in the hallway for her wrap to be taken. And flowers literally bloomed in every imaginable corner—garlands, wreaths, sprays—all mingling their fragrence with the ladies' perfumes. Flowers, a myriad candles, the sound of the orchestra playing softly—all the young ladies were intoxicated before their first sips of champagne!

The receiving line was formed inside the entrance to the ballroom itself, where the Carlyle butler stood to announce each distinguished guest. "Baron and Lady von Hustings, Lady Evaline von Hustings. Lord Ian Clarahan, Earl of Islington, Lady Clarahan, Miss Rachel Clarahan. Squire and Mrs. Jonathan Whitson, Misses Lorinda, Lucinda and Annabelle Whitson. Captain John Hildreth." And on and on, through every rank of nobility up to prince, with a Scottish laird and a Russian countess there by luck, house guests of other guests, down through the rural gentry of squires and plain misters. Each guest was greeted with the same warm smile by the Duchess, who looked stunning in her gown of sapphire blue. The hem of her gown was cleverly embroidered in diamanté, patterned to repeat the swirls of her diamond and sapphire necklace. Her hair was done up high under a tiara, set with one large diamond at the centre. Her blue eyes sparkled with the darker reflections from her gown, and her clear skin was almost white next to the blue, except for the blush of colour at her cheeks. Her charming smile was renewed for each visitor, through curtsey after curtsey, compliment after compliment.

The Duke had been standing by his wife's side to receive their guests but excused himself early on to host those already assembled in the game room which, he said, would be less taxing to his newly recouped strength than standing around half the night. This left the Marquis on his mother's other side to bow over so many gloved hands. He was pleased at first to accept the compliments, on his mother's behalf, of what a fine picture they made. Indeed, they were a handsome couple with their matching blond hair, his in curls, hers in sleek twists. He was dressed in formal black and white, with the exception of his waistcoat, which was a blue that matched his mother's dress, but in velvet, with silver embroidery. The white of his cravat was interrupted by a diamond-headed stickpin, set with tiny sapphires. Carleton, glancing from the line of guests to the Duchess, was thinking that he could be content with a woman like his mother, if only one existed.

He had started the evening with a confident smile and a friendly enough greeting to anyone he actually knew. As the time wore on, however, and an appalling number of identical-looking young women were paraded past him, his smile turned almost wooden, his welcomes to mere "Howdoyoudo's?" and his thoughts to those of desertion—or patricide!

The young women all looked the same, he thought with dismay. Whose idea was it to dress every debutante in white or the most faded-looking pastels? It only served to make the brunettes' complexions seem muddy and the blondes' look sallow. Most of them greeted him with their eyes on his shoes, so he did not even know what they looked like. How was he going to put a name and a face together to ask one to dance?

There was no need to worry yet, he was relieved to learn as the receiving line dwindled. The first dance was arranged for him with his cousin Margaret since, the

Duchess explained, that seemed the most comfortable way to open the ball, without having to bother about titles and ranks. She squeezed his arm and left him to go make introductions among the young people. He could see his own chums and many of the fellows in scarlet uniforms already paired off, ready to do their duty as soon as he took the floor. *Ave Caesar*, he repeated silently to himself as he crossed the room to his aunt and Margaret by her side. He had time to notice how fine his cousin looked, even if she was wearing white lace, and told his aunt so, winning at least two friends in the lion's den.

"No, Maggie, I meant it," he went on as she took his arm and they walked to the centre of the floor. "Damn, but my own cousin is the prettiest girl here! What luck!"

"Have you seen Robert this evening?" Margaret grew serious as the music started.

"Your brother Robert?"

"Of course my brother Robert! Don't be dense. Have you seen him?"

"Yes, his collar is too high. The boy is turning into a regular Tulip. But what is this all about?"

"Well, I have to ask a favour, for him, since he obviously has not. Do you mind?"

"How should I know if I mind until I know the favour? Come, Maggie, out with it; what scrape are you two involved in now?"

"No, Cousin Alexander, it's nothing like that! It's about a girl, a Miss Sophie Devenance. Robert wishes—prays—that you please not ask her to dance with you this evening."

"Goodness, child, is my reputation so bad? I don't even know Miss Sophie Devenance!"

"Yes, but Robert does! He is going to offer for her soon, and that is why you mustn't dance with her!"

"I may be dense, Maggie, but why shouldn't I dance with Robert's intended? I would like to know the girl who is to become my cousin."

"But, Alexander, don't you see; if you ask Miss Devenance to dance, she will never be permitted to accept Robert until you marry. If there is the least possibility of your offering for—"

Carleton missed a step. "My God, is it as bad as that? Do they *all* know? I must be a laughing-stock!"

"No one is making fun, Cousin Alexander, but only a fool would not see the opportunity, so please, will you do Robert this favour? It means a great deal to him."

"Surely, Margaret, and with my blessings, if you could just point her out for me—No, I take it she is the blonde beauty dancing with Robert now, for the looks they are exchanging are positively sickening."

"Yes, that is Miss Devenance, and Robert will be much relieved. I told him he could count on you, if you only knew how things stood."

The music stopped and Carleton took Margaret's arm to lead her back to her mother. Margaret looked up to see one corner of his mouth twitching with a smile, and the merriment returned to his blue eyes. "Of course," he said, "just as I know I can count on you, for I have a favour to ask in return—Maggie, will you marry me?"

"But, Cousin, this is my engagement ball!" Margaret replied, then giggled in a manner quite unsuitable for an affianced lady, as her mother's reproving expression reminded her. "Poor Cousin Alexander, is it so awful?" she asked seriously. "I am sure I must know some one or two women you could—" She turned to scan the room but was interrupted by Carleton's, "Oh, no, you don't! I have enough matchmakers around me now. I'll pick my own partners, thank you."

Even that amount of dignity was to be denied him, he realised as his mother appeared at his elbow, making him known to Miss Althea Chasmont, at which his breeding forced him to ask that young lady to dance.

Miss Chasmont, Carleton learned from his questions, was the niece of a neighbouring baronet. Yes, she liked to dance; no, it was not too warm. Carleton ransacked his mind to find a topic for conversation since Miss Chasmont was obviously not willing—or able—to make the effort. Gods, he thought, what *are* young women interested in? The ones he knew concerned themselves with love, money and gossip, none suitable here. Before the silence could grow more embarrassing for them both, he complimented Miss Chasmont for not being one of those females who ruined the pleasure of the dance with incessant chatter. Her "Thank you, my Lord" took care of the rest of the dance. Carleton had, of course, to find Miss Chasmont's aunt and return the young lady to her side, where, just as surely, his own mother was waiting.

The young lady offered to him this time had a sweet smile, but she could not dance. Their attempts to find mutual acquaintances in London were constantly interrupted with her apologies, his claims of fault, her demurrals.

"Well, shall we stand aside for a moment or two?" he finally asked in desperation and was rewarded with another of the sweet smiles. Conversation went somewhat better— her elder brother having been some four years behind Carleton at Eton—until the music stopped. The Marquis looked hopefully for one of his friends, but none was close by so he had to go through the routine again and again, greeting his mother after each dance with noticeably less enthusiasm. There was the young woman whose nose was her best feature, thankfully separating her eyes; the one who stammered and blushed the whole dance; the one so bedecked with flowers that he could hardly get through some of the dance steps without mangling a posy.

His last partner before dinner was the prettiest of the lot and the most talkative, if an inquisition was a form of communication. Hoping to please him by showing interest in his home, he charitably assumed, and not for baser reasons, she quizzed him on the age of the Hall, who designed which wing, when the title had been conferred.

Carleton had some vague knowledge of all this but not enough to satisfy Miss Smythe-Warner's curiosity. Luckily it was a country dance, so changing partners granted him a reprieve.

When the figures of the dance brought his cousin Margaret to his side—not entirely by chance, as he had purposely joined her set—he was desperate.

"Maggie, sweet cousin, if you won't marry me, at least go down to supper with me."

"But I can't, Cousin Alexander, I am promised to Mark for supper. Besides, Father is going to announce the engagement at supper! Isn't there anyone else you could ask?"

His humourless smile was her only answer as he returned to his original partner for the closing bars of the dance, his mind working feverishly. He could see his mother with a cluster of women at the ballroom's exit nearest the library—and then, inspiration! Miss Smythe-Warner was promptly returned to her mama, with his promise to research the history of the castle for her. Before his mother could get a word in, he muttered something about family records... library, at once... mustn't wait for him, he'd be down directly, and disappeared down the hall and through the library door.

# SIX

"Whew!" Carleton took a deep breath in relief. He leaned against the library's door and wiped his face.

"Congratulations on your escape," said a soft voice from shadows across the room, followed by an amused little laugh.

Carleton's dismay was genuine. "I am sorry to intrude, madam, I shall leave at once. I did not expect this room to be occupied."

"No, don't go. Of course you would not think the library occupied, not with so many empty heads hanging about. Oh, perhaps I should not have spoken. You are not a friend of Lord Carleton's, are you? No, I see you are no London Dandy, all done up in frills and glitter."

"Thank you, ma'am, and no, I am, um, not exactly a friend of Carleton's. But you have an advantage on me, madam; won't you come into the light?" he asked as he moved farther into the room.

She put a book down on a side table and took a step or two forward, moving her hand from the candle it was shielding. Carleton was dumbfounded. Where had this— this stranger come from? She was small and brown-haired, with a turned-up nose and no great beauty—in fact, her looks were out of favour with the current concept of prettiness—but there was so much that was unique about her that Carleton could only stare for a minute. For one thing, her colouring was downright healthy, no, not sun-coarsened, only fresh, alive. Her hair had glimmers of gold in it which could only have come from sunshine. Her gown reinforced the whole image; a lively, happy yellow, it was completely unornamented except for a single silk daisy at the center of the décolletage. The gown was gathered under the small bust, then fell straight to the floor Another daisy tied in a long yellow ribbon of the same material caught the curls at the back of her head. What was most surprising, however, was that she was looking him straight in the eyes and laughing happily from a full, generous mouth, not blushing at his admittedly rude stare, or tongue-tied with shyness.

"You see?" She laughed. "Not your delicate English rose, only a common countryside daisy, so you need not flee from me, too."

"Most assuredly anything but common," he said, the first thing which came to his extremely bewildered mind. Surely he must have noticed anyone as lovely as this on the receiving line! Who in the world was she, and where was her chaperone, and, most of all, whatever was she doing in the library alone with him? "Please forgive my impertinence, but most of the company has repaired to dinner, and I am sure your mother must be worried over you. May I escort you to her?"

"Oh, no, it is Aunt Claudia who is my chaperone—my mother is long dead—and I assure you that my aunt has completely forgotten my existence. She deposited me at the side of a veritable dragon and immediately found the whist tables. No, she will only recall that I made her arrive so late she missed some time playing. There will be no dragging her from the tables for hours, so here I am, unconventional as it may seem. I did say I was repairing a flounce." And dimples appeared at the sides of her mouth as she unconcernedly sat down in one of the leather chairs.

Unconventional was not the word Carleton would have used, for the exquisitely simple gown hugging her perfect figure had not a single flounce, frill or furbelow to its design. Besides, chaperones existed solely to protect such innocence from ones like himself! Carleton knew that his very presence would compromise her reputation, even if she was not aware of it. He looked into wide brown eyes filled with dancing gold specks and forced himself to try again. "I am certain even Aunt Claudia could not approve of your being closeted in the library with me," he said bluntly, thinking to himself, what an understatement.

"Well, then I won't tell her! Will you? No, I see you are much too kind for that. Even if she does hear of it, I am sure it can't signify. She believes in the prevailing philosophy: If you don't think about something, it does not exist. That way she banishes all unpleasantness. Like some demented Descartes, *non cogito, ergo nihil!*"

"Never tell me you read philosophy," Carleton exclaimed, smiling in spite of himself. "That's doing it too strong."

"Why, sir, didn't you study philosophy? My father used to instruct me and talk about what interested him. I must confess not much comes my way since his death, and I never did appreciate Aristotle, in spite of my father's wishes."

"In the Greek, I suppose?" Carleton asked, finally taking a seat near hers, resolved that in for a penny, in for a pound. Supper would take nearly an hour, at least, and he would enjoy this unique company while he could and worry about extricating himself later. He deserved that much of a reprieve, he felt.

"Aunt Claudia would certainly be furious with me now, you know," said the young lady, not appearing to worry over that at all. "She practically ordered me not to appear bookish to anyone, but, yes, Papa had me taught Greek, and Latin, and all the things he was taught." The dimples reappeared. "Lest you think me unnatural, he also found someone to teach me embroidery!"

Carleton laughed out loud, for the first time this evening, he realised. "Your father must have been an interesting man, Miss . . . Miss . . . ?"

"Bethingame, Miss Elizabeth Bethingame. And you, sir?"

"I . . . I am still wondering why you were not in the ballroom." Carleton redirected the conversation quickly, trying to cover his evasion. "You are obviously dressed for a ball, to be seen and admired, so why are you in the library? No one has offended you, I trust?"

"Yes, you could easily be a knight come to rescue a lady in distress," she said seriously, studying his face. Then she remembered his question. "This whole ball offends me! I know I must take Ellie's gown out to be admired, but—No, I see you do not understand, and I am sure you do not wish to hear my problems. Yours must be equally as pressing, to remove you from the company in such a manner."

"No, I assure you, Miss Bethingame, my difficulties were only temporary. Please go on, perhaps I might find a way to be of assistance, shining armour or not." He assumed she was going to confess something about strait-ened circumstances, borrowed clothes, an orphan's plight. He smiled encouragingly.

"How kind you are!" She gave him a grateful look, which aroused his sympathies even more, until she started to speak. "It's those wretched Carletons and their high-handed summons, as though we were all cattle at auction, to be inspected by their lordling before purchase! Aunt Claudia pestered me to death—even threatening to call Uncle Aubry down on me—until I agreed to come. Then Ellie felt it would do *her* good, so I had to stand for endless fittings, wasting even more time. You see, Ellie is now Mademoiselle Elena, but she used to be my governess's niece until my father sent her to study under Monsieur Blanc. She had so much talent it would have been wasted as a country seamstress. Now she is trying to establish a clientele in London, and if I was seen in one of her creations and—and *took*—it must reflect on her. Only I do not wish to be noticed, and I refuse to have anything to do with this—this shopping expedition to find Lord Alexander a proper wife."

Carleton's anger was in danger of reaching epic proportions—at his family, all gossips in general, and this righteous little hell-cat in particular. Thinking to take her down a peg, he asked, "What makes you think that Lord Carleton would be so interested in you that you have to hide in the library?"

"I am not hiding, merely waiting for the proper moment." Her chin went up and her eyes flashed. "Carleton would be interested in the Folly, all right, unless he is a ninny like the rest of them out there. That is Bething's Folly," she went on, fiercely, proudly, "the finest stud farm in the county and soon in the country."

Carleton's anger was replaced by amazement. The girl was so unselfconscious she didn't even realise what a stir she herself would make, reserving her pride for a piece of property. Now he placed the name, and the Folly, and was interested indeed! Old Lord Bethingame had been a completely indifferent farmer but an avid horseman, not for hunting but for racing. He had visions of the scientific selection of studs and mares, improved conditions for foaling and training colts, champion lines of winning horses and dynasties of expensive offspring. He sold off huge plots of Bething Manor's unproductive acreage, keeping only what he needed to raise fodder and for pasturage. He went completely into debt to renovate his barns and stables, to purchase blood stock. No one thought he could make a go of it and some considered him crazy, calling his scheme Bething's Folly. The name must have stuck, although Carleton believed he had heard of some fine horses coming from the stud recently. He did not recall anything about Lady Bethingame, but he was aware that Lord Bethingame had died some years before. Carleton had never concerned himself with the Folly beyond that, even though it was within an hour's ride of Carlyle Hall. His father would know the complete history, he was sure, and Margaret must be of an age with Miss Bethingame, and he planned to make enquiries. In the meantime he could not help asking the lady herself if she was perhaps betrothed to someone else that made the high-handed Lord Carleton so ineligible a suitor for her—and Bething's Folly. She was not betrothed, she declared indignantly, and astonished him even further by stating her intention to remain unwed.

"But Miss Bethingame, surely you cannot run the place alone, and must eventually wed anyway..."

"You are sounding suspiciously like Uncle Aubry," obviously no compliment. "I am nineteen, sir, and have been managing Bething's Folly for two years now. We are beginning to show a profit. We have excellent prospects for this year and great plans for the future. Do you think I would let my father's dream become a rich man's plaything, or be sold to pay a poor one's gambling debts?"

Carleton considered. Under English law, a woman's property did become her husband's at marriage, to do with what he would, so he had to acknowledge Miss Bethingame's statements. He just could not believe some handsome young fellow had not come along to change her mind.

"And Uncle Aubry?" he asked.

"He is furious the Folly didn't come to him along with the title, though he never approved of it in the first place. He is positive I cannot manage it, even when he sees that I can. Furthermore, he sees no reason to bother with my welfare and is determined to marry me off—most likely for a handsome settlement—to a widower friend in Lancashire who needs a mother for his three children. The widower is not even interested in racing." That was truly a scathing denunciaton, from Miss Bethingame's tone of voice.

"But I take it Uncle Aubry is your guardian," Carleton insisted. "Surely he can force you to wed, or take over the Folly if he really feels it would be in your best interest?" Carleton was truly curious, and the girl responded, treating him like a co-conspirator.

44

"He has threatened to try, but my father's will was very explicit: The Folly is mine, to own and to manage. He trusted me. I have hired lawyers to look into that very thing, and they tell me that if I keep proper records and do not go any further into debt, then Uncle Aubry has no claims. As for marriage, I do not believe even Uncle Aubry would carry me to the altar, kicking and screaming. Could you see the stir it would make?"

The Marquis could, and he could even sympathise as she went on to explain the difficulties she would be in if Carleton *did* offer for her, for her uncle would have apoplexy if she refused. He might even attempt to have her declared mentally incompetent! This only recalled to mind Carleton's own difficulties, and especially the situation he had got himself into now, accepting the child's confidences. He smiled at the thought. This "child" was running a successful horse farm and had more control over her life than he had of his!

She smiled back at him, and again he marvelled that her warmth was so genuine, that there was no artistry or flirting. He was about to ease into a confession when Ferddie Milbrooke burst into the room.

"Oh, there you are, Carleton! The Duchess is in a rare pet, you know, supper and all. Sent me to find you, in no uncertain terms." He came farther into the room and saw Miss Bethingame, who was suddenly on her feet, her fists clenched and her eyes flashing sparks. Ferddie slowly raised his quizzing glass, not looking at Carleton at all or noting his frantic signals. "Trust you to find the needle in the haystack, Carleton," he finally drawled. Then, as the circumstances dawned on him—the closed door, Carleton not down to supper—a frown of doubt appeared on his forehead and he forgot the affected manner of speech. "You know, it's not at all the thing for you to be here like this, if you don't mind me saying so. I can't think it's—"

"No, it is *not* at all the thing for me to be here with such a deceitful, despicable, d-d-dastardly cur like you!" the girl

45

finally sputtered at Carleton. Then, to Ferddie, "Good evening, sir."

Ferddie's mouth hung open and his glass dropped to the end of its ribbon, but he had sense enough to open the door for the lady before she kicked it down, as she looked very tempted to do. He put his hand on Carleton's shoulder as the Marquis would have gone after her.

"No, Carleton, I don't know what went on in here—and I don't want to, either—but unless you mean to offer for the chit, you'd best not be seen leaving here with her."

"Right, Ferddie, and I congratulate you on your wisdom! What did you think of her?"

"She seemed to have a deal of, um, spirit," Ferddie answered uncertainly.

"Yes, like a regular she-cat, or kitten."

Ferddie looked closely at his friend's smile to find the usual sarcasm, but there was none. He decided it would be best to keep his thoughts to himself until he saw which way the wind blew; but for a change it was Milbrooke who wore the know-it-all expression and Carleton who had a friendly smile when they left the library together some few minutes later.

The Duchess was standing near the ballroom door with some friends when they entered. She sent an I'll-speak-to-you-later look toward her son and pointedly asked if he had found what he was looking for in the library.

"Yes, your Grace," he answered pleasantly, "I believe I have found it now."

The Duchess raised her eyebrows but asked no further questions. She turned to present a Miss Winston to him—and to Ferddie, whose wrist was somehow curiously caught in the Marquis's grip. They made their bows and, the grip tightening until realisation came, Ferddie asked the young lady to dance. Miss Winston was relieved, for like most of the other debutantes, she found the Marquis's chiseled features and cold blue eyes intimidating, while Ferddie's ruddy good looks were much more comfortable. Miss

Winston's mother was annoyed. The Duchess was neither dismayed nor disappointed to see her son walk off, scanning the room. She was only extremely curious, as was almost every other pair of eyes in the entire ballroom.

Carleton realised that he was the object of a great deal of speculation, but there was no help for it. He also realised it would not enhance his apology to Miss Bethingame to draw so much unwelcome attention, just what she particularly wished to avoid. He was not about to let her disappear before he could make amends, however. He had had a glimpse of something precious and knew he mustn't lose it. There she was now, he saw, a glimmer of bright yellow in a far corner, sitting behind an enormous dowager in purple satin with an ostrich headdress. Somewhere on his way across the endless-seeming room, Miss Bethingame became aware of his approach. A hanky in her hand was suffering sadly, and her colouring suddenly lost its rosy glow, betraying her; but her eyes were fixed on the floor, almost the only ones in the room not on Carleton, which brought a smile back to his lips. How fierce she looked, he thought, and how exquisite, under all the lights of the ballroom where he could really appreciate her clear skin and the gold in her brown hair. Truly she was like a wildflower, all the more lovely for bravely growing where one least expected it.

Miss Elizabeth Bethingame, meanwhile, was horrified. She was still furious over Carleton's behaviour, of course, but she was also mortified at her own. She kept repeating to herself all the awful things she had said about him and his family—and he was actually in front of her! How dare he?

"Miss Bethingame," Carleton started, only to be met with that same "How dare you?" so he dispensed with the courtesies, drew a chair up and seated himself. The dowager in purple sniffed and muttered something about unmannerly young people until she was quelled by a look from the Marquis and turned away.

"Miss Bethingame, please listen to me. My actions were

47

deplorable, I know. I also know you would not have spoken to me if you knew the truth, so what was I to do?"

"You *might* have stopped me from saying those things about you!"

"Why? They were true, mostly, except that I like this ball as little as you do. Please believe me, I would not have made such a spectacle of myself!"

She looked at him closely, positive his smooth insincerity would show. Instead, all she noticed were how blue his eyes were, how strong his chin, which did nothing to ease her mind, nor did his lopsided smile. Her lips twitched to return it, but she recalled her situation and firmed her shoulders resolutely.

"And now, sir, you are making a spectacle of me by sitting here!"

"Something else I must apologise for, though also not to my liking. You must admit I could not apologise for my first fault without committing this second! Besides, the damage is done and the music is starting, so may I have the pleasure of this dance?"

Miss Bethingame had already noticed the orchestra beginning after the dinner intermission, a waltz, to her dismay. "No thank you, my Lord, I do not care to waltz," she said coldly.

Carleton was puzzled, for he thought he was resolving the library difficulty as gracefully as possible. He was also not used to being refused and did not care for what a fool he might seem to the company, so he spoke more bitingly than he might have.

"What, Miss Bethingame, growing missish? I did not think a mere waltz would daunt you, not after your previous behaviour, which must shock everyone in this room!" He sought to defeat her feeble excuse and succeeded.

"My Lord Carleton, I would not dance with you if you were the only man here, waltz or not!" she answered just as angrily, her temper as short-fused as his, he was astonished to see. Most well-bred ladies were taught not to show their emotions and seldom did, except for weeping or swooning. He seriously doubted Miss Bethingame would do either. This reflection gave him time to gather his own self-control and realise further how unlike other women Miss Bethingame actually was.

"Well, then may I find you a partner for the dance?" he asked in an effort to regain a little favour. "At least then you might have the pleasure of the waltz, to save what must be a dismal evening for you." He rose as if to leave, but a small hand reached for his sleeve.

"Please, my Lord, I . . . I do not waltz," she said in a barely audible voice, and, yes, Miss Bethingame was blushing.

"Do you mean you don't know how?" asked Carleton bluntly, unbelievingly. This girl-woman could speak Greek and run an estate—yet she did not know how to waltz. Her tiny nod confirmed this and brought him an unexpected rush of relief that her refusal was for the dance, not him. This was quickly replaced by regret over his own words.

"I am sorry to have teased you, Miss Bethingame— Lord, I seem constantly to be apologising! I swear, I do not usually make such a muddle of things. Please, may I fetch you some champagne or lemonade? Perhaps something to eat, since you did not go to supper? No? Do you wish me to find your aunt so you may leave, for you have been noticed enough, I am sure, even for Ellie and Uncle Aubry."

Her features relaxed a little as she thanked him for the thought, but said she doubted her aunt would leave the card rooms voluntarily for she got so few chances to indulge in her favourite pastime.

"Even if I were to say you had the headache?"

"Aunt Claudia would know it was a hum; I've never had a headache in my life."

"But if I had a servant bring the message, she could not very well deny it in front of the whole company, could she?"

Miss Bethingame smiled for the first time since leaving

the library, a tentative, appreciative smile that aroused feelings of tenderness Carleton hadn't known he possessed. A servant was sent to the card rooms, another to fetch the ladies' pelisses and call for the carriage, while Lord Carleton and Miss Bethingame circled the dancers on the way out. The lady was uneasy to be under the scrutiny of everyone along the walls, though she was thankful to be leaving an entirely unfortunate affair. The gentleman, meanwhile, was delighted to help her vanish before the dance was over for more subtle reasons. Carleton knew he could not ask her to dance again without causing even more comment, and he did not trust his friends! It was as simple as that: if he could not have her company, no one would.

Aunt Claudia, Lady Burke, a short, very plump woman of middle age, was waiting in the hall. She was introduced to Lord Carleton as Miss Bethingame's father's sister, widow of the late Lord Humphreys Burke. Carleton immediately volunteered to express her regrets to the Duchess, so there was no question of their staying on, to Aunt Claudia's irritation. She was not about to ask her niece for an explanation in his presence, either, so she merely noted Miss Bethingame's continued healthful appearance before moving disgustedly through the front doors. Before Miss Bethingame could follow, Carleton pulled a flower from a vase on the hall table and handed it to her, saying, "Miss Bethingame, I am truly sorry if I have hurt you."

She said nothing but gave him a fleeting, radiant smile before running through the door after her aunt.

The ballroom was buzzing with talk now between dances. Carleton reintroduced himself to the first girl he saw and asked her for the next country dance, just forming. He chatted pleasantly to her, and successive changes of partners, about the weather, the countryside, the war in France. What was so hard about this? he wondered. He danced continuously through the second part of the ball and was gracious to all of his partners, selecting them by nearness to hand and finding something to compliment each one about: this one's gown, that one's dancing or flowers or green eyes. Previously awkward, shy girls blossomed to lay their hearts at his feet. It was only as the last dance was announced, the second waltz, that Carleton stood aside. He looked around slowly and many breaths were held in anticipation to see whom he would honour. His mother looked at him quizzically as he walked toward her from nearby, but he did not select any of the debutantes at her side to partner. Instead, he made an exquisite low bow in front of the Duchess and held out his hand. "Your Grace, may I have this dance with the most beautiful woman in the ballroom?"

# SEVEN

Breakfast on the morning following the ball was a haphazard affair. Many of the guests rose early, ate hurriedly and departed in order to arrive in London that evening, having made their farewells the night before. Among these were most of Carleton's own friends, with wagers on who could arrive at White's first. Only Ferddie Milbrooke was staying on for another week. The other house guests were planning to leave Carlyle Hall after luncheon, put up at posting house inns and conclude their journeys the following day; they were resting late this morning in preparation. The Duke had eaten much earlier and was with his estate manager, a servant informed his son, who was relieved that his father had not over-taxed himself with the evening. The Duchess was not yet down, he was told, and would breakfast in her rooms, which also relieved Carleton. He had no wish to face her enquiries yet. In fact, he had no desire to face the remaining guests at all, certainly not the same young ladies with the same conversations and the same hopeful mamas. With this and other thoughts in mind, he asked Ferddie to accompany him on a ride. While Ferddie changed his clothes, Carleton went to the stables. He ordered up his own horse, Jupiter, and a mount for Milbrooke, then sought out his father's head groom. Old Nate knew more about horses than anyone else in Carleton's acquaintance and had lived his entire life in the region of

Carlyle Hall. What he had to say about Bething's Folly only raised Carleton's interest. In Nate's opinion, there was a good man running the place, and the Duke could very well consider some of the new-fangled ideas there since they seemed to be getting the Folly better yearlings every season. Ferddie returned to hear a discussion of the lineage of the Bethingame stable and the coming prospects. He kept his silence until he and Carleton were mounted and on their way out of the stable yard when he asked, "Any place in particular you'd have in mind to ride, Carleton?"

The Marquis looked back over his shoulder and saw his friend's wide smile. "Don't you tease me with it, Ferddie; I'll have enough of that later." He let the eager Jupiter have his head and galloped off down the drive, Ferddie close behind him.

The approach to Bething Manor was up a narrow dirt lane with trees arching over, dappling the sunlight. At the end of the lane stood worn stone columns and, past them on either side of the carriage drive, green lawn and a border garden filled with the gentle colours of early spring blooms. The manor itself stood in the full sun, its grey stone exterior softened by ivy creepers and forsythia bushes.It was a modest, solid house with casement windows and neat chimneys at either end, obviously built with an eye toward practicality and comfort, without the sprawling hodge-podge of ornamental architecture so common—and so hard to keep warm. Beyond the grass verge to one side of the house was what appeared to be a formal garden, and to the other, up a small rise, a long, low structure of the same grey stone, surrounded by perimeters of neat white fencing as far as the eye could see, with here and there an outbuilding or cottage. Everything was immaculate and in perfect order, not a fence post tilting, not a fallen tree branch in sight. Horses—mares with foals—could be seen in the distance, on the hills behind the house and stable, and noises of some activity were coming from behind the latter;

otherwise all was quiet, with no one in sight and nothing but soft chimney smoke and bird song to give the place an almost breathtakingly beautiful pastoral charm, a great sense of peace and contentment.

He could well understand Miss Bethingame's determination to keep the Folly, Carleton thought, for it justified her pride and reflected her devotion in every neat hedge, every foal cavorting in the sunshine on the hills. Then he laughed to himself and shook his head ruefully: Interest in the estate was the last thing he could afford to express. At least his curiosity about the Folly was satisfied; now he would see if his last night's impressions were correct.

No one came to take the horses, so after they had dismounted Ferddie held the reins while Carleton lifted the knocker on the wide oak door. After a few moments the door was opened by an elderly man in shirt sleeves with a polishing cloth in one hand. The staff at Bething Manor was obviously not used to receiving unexpected callers. One glance at the visitors, however, their elegant coats, their polished Hessians, to say nothing of their fine horses and stylish good looks, and the butler accurately determined their social importance. He immediately summoned a footman to lead the horses to the stables and drew himself up to accept the gentlemen's cards with all the dignity of his breed, despite his informal appearance. He led them to a small sitting room off the front hall while he went to announce them to Lady Burke, who he assured them was at home.

"Peculiar household, don't you think?" Ferddie asked, wandering around the small room whose furnishings were a little worn, the draperies somewhat faded.

Carleton made no answer, trying to visualise this as a setting for the girl he had met last night. Yes, he could see her here, her honest, outspoken ways matching the sturdy, comfortable furnishings, her unaffected loveliness recalled by the wildflowers collected in simple glass vases. He smiled, amused by his own romanticising. He was making too much of last night's encounter. Surely Miss Bethingame would turn out to be a pretty enough country miss with the same cloying agreeableness of all the others, or a spoiled, demanding beauty, like so many of the London Incomparables. She would be as selfishly two-faced as any other woman when it suited her. Still, he could not help his eager anticipation when the butler returned, this time with formal coat buttoned and gloves on.

"Lady Burke would be honoured to receive you," he said. "Will you follow me?" He spoke with perfect composure, not reflecting the turmoil these two guests' arrival had created in the drawing room.

Lady Burke was there dithering around the room, straightening pillows and searching for somewhere to stash the disreputable novel she'd been reading. She finally shoved it into a sewing basket, muttering the whole time about Aubry's business, and there, didn't she just know it, and where was Elizabeth? This was how Carleton and Milbrooke found her when the butler opened the door and stood aside. She was talking to herself, they realised, unless one counted the small, ancient pug at her side. This creature, as squat and plump as its mistress, instantly set to yapping when they entered the room, and trundled toward them as fast as its little bowed legs could carry it to commence snapping at their boots. Its snarling attack made greetings and introductions impossible; Lady Burke's oh dear's helped not at all, and the butler had disappeared. In desperation Carleton reached out to a side table near the doorway, where they still stood, and took a bon-bon from a dish. He rolled it across the floor, just past the pug's nose. The dog waddled over to the treat, then darted between its mistress's feet with it, as though to eat in a safe spot. At least it had finally quieted. Lady Burke gathered the dog to her cushiony bosom with a few bad doggie's and oh my's and at last remembered to invite her guests to be seated. She chose a sofa, with the pug up next to her. Ferddie selected a seat as far away as was polite, once he had been introduced.

"Lady Burke," Carleton began in as reasonably steady a voice as he could muster after that interlude, "I hope we are not intruding, but we have called to enquire after your niece. We pray she has recovered from her headache of last night?"

"Headache? The girl's never had a headache! Well, maybe with the measles, but, let me tell you, it was something else on her mind, one of her racketty notions.... Oh, dear, perhaps I should not have said that." Here Lady Burke frowned, but then her round face brightened as she found a solution. "Well, um, perhaps one of her notions did give her the headache last night. Yes, I am sure of it! Of course, she is very well this morning. That is, I think she is...." And here dismay mingled with uncertainty in her expression.

Carleton was saved from having to reply to this bewildering speech by the return of the butler, who was bearing a tray of decanters and glasses. Behind him a footman carried tea things over to Lady Burke.

After Carleton had been served and the butler turned to Ferddie, the Marquis could not help overhearing Lady Burke's nervous whisperings to the footman, whose sleeve she pulled at to punctuate her urgency: "John, listen to me, you must find Miss Elizabeth! She'll be at the dratted stables, so run! Tell her it is an emergency, tell her anything but get her here!"

John looked hurriedly at the guests to see if his mistress was in any immediate danger, then quickly departed, to the butler's surprise and displeasure as he turned around to find his assistant gone without having passed any refreshments. He did so himself with resigned dignity, then asked if there would be anything else.

"No, that will be all, Taylor, thank you. That is, I think so. Yes, well Elizabeth will be coming shortly." Lady Burke firmly addressed this last to Carleton, although she followed it with a barely audible muttering: "Gads, I hope so! Having to fetch her out of the stables now . . . if she'll come. Aubry will just have to see . . ." She was meanwhile buttering a muffin fastidiously, which she then fed piece by piece to the fat little dog next to her.

Carleton wondered what had her so fidgety, whether it was his presence, fear of the threatening Uncle Aubry, or, worst of all, her niece's unpredictable temperament. It must be a combination of all three, he decided, if not her own eccentric nature. Eccentric, hell, he amended. Miss Bethingame's aunt was decidedly screw-loose! What an environment for a young girl! To make some effort at conversation, he asked Lady Burke how she had done at the card tables the night before, which turned out to be a brilliant stroke on his part. The lady brightened immediately and went into a lengthy, detailed description of her partners, her hands, the particulars of the betting. Carleton only had to nod or murmur agreement, so he was free to reflect on other things, like what in the world he was doing here, and how treacherous friends could be at times. Ferddie Milbrooke had not said ten words since their arrival, only sitting there with a saintly smile on his face, enjoying the whole preposterous scene immeasurably. Most likely memorizing it, Carleton fumed, to taunt him with it later. The Marquis glared over at his friend, who merely raised his glass in a mock salute.

Lady Burke was running down, beginning to lament her early departure from the cards, when a door to the rear of the house was slammed. "Oh, dear Lord" was the last thing she said before boots were heard running down the hall, and a fierce scrabbling, and hopefully reassuring calls of "Aunt Claudia, I'm coming!"

They could hear the butler coming down the front hall: "Miss Elizabeth, wait! Don't!" met by shouts from the back hall: "Taylor, Aunt Claudia!"

Milbrooke and Carleton were on their feet by now, facing the door and expecting who knows what when it burst open and Miss Bethingame rushed in, followed by the butler, the footman, a small man in rough clothes and a large, muddy, spanielly-looking dog. The pug on the couch took one look at this last intruder and bounded off on a ferocious-sounding but completely ludicrous attack. The spaniel began darting around the room, barking joyfully at this new game. Lady Burke took one look at her niece— high boots, woolen shirt knotted at the waist and britches— and fainted dead away on the sofa.

Miss Bethingame glanced at Ferddie, whose mouth was hanging open in stupefaction, then turned to Carleton, knowing immediately what had happened. She directed one scathing word at him—*"You!"*—before hurrying to her aunt's side.

The tea table went over with a crash and yelping. The pug withdrew from battle in a fit of wheezing; the spaniel kept up its excited barking; Lady Burke moaned.

Miss Bethingame reached for a pillow to put under her aunt's head, then turned to face Carleton, her eyes sparking fire, her fists clenched. "If I were a man I would call you out, you . . . you . . ."

"Miss Bitsy!" The third man cut her off before she could find a terrible enough word, which only redirected her anger at himself.

"If you ever call me that again, Robbie Jackson, I'll have you turned out of here, so help me I—"

"Down, sir, down!" Ferddie was shouting at the spaniel leaving muddy footprints on his pants, and "Grab his collar, you fool," at the footman gingerly trying to corner the delighted animal. The pug was in such a state its eyes looked about to pop out of its head, and the butler was no better off. Carleton could feel the laughter bubbling up and fought to keep the urge contained. With only the slightest bit of humour in his voice he took command of the situation, issuing orders like a general deploying his forces:

"Taylor is it? Please fetch Lady Burke's woman and someone to pick up the mess here. Milbrooke, Mr. Jackson here could relieve you of that beast if you would follow him to the stables. And you," he said to the footman, bending down to lift up the asthmatic old pug and holding it out at arm's length, "kindly remove this creature. I believe cold milk is what my aunt gave hers in this condition.... They will know in the kitchen."

When they were all gone, Carleton turned to Miss Bethingame, now fanning her aunt with a newspaper. He took another, better look at her appearance—the loose brown braid hanging down her back, the dirt smudges on her face, and most of all the britches—and one corner of his mouth twitched up. No wonder her aunt was so addlepated, raising such a madcap; but, yes, she was as adorable as he remembered, even mad and messy. He could not help it but a low chuckle broke the silence after the pandemonium, and, finally, uncontrollable laughter. Miss Bethingame was ready to make a furious rejoinder to this last insult when something in his laughter stopped her. He was not exactly laughing at her, her instincts told her—he was much too well-bred for that—only at the hopelessly absurd situation. Her own good-humoured sense of the ridiculous took over and she joined him in genuine amusement until her aunt groaned again on the sofa.

"It is fine to laugh, my Lord, but look at all the trouble I am in now," she said seriously. "Would you please leave before my aunt regains her senses?"

"My leaving would only make things worse, I should think. If you will change to, ah, more suitable attire we may all reassemble and pass the incident off as nothing exceptional. As you said last night, if we do not discuss it, it never happened. At least we will delay your aunt's scolding."

Miss Bethingame had to acknowledge the wisdom of his advice. There was no other choice besides, for he was making no effort to depart and here was the maid with the smelling salts and vinaigrette. It would be too cruel to make

Aunt Claudia face Carleton alone again, so she told the maid to stay until her return and hurried past the Marquis, who nodded reassuringly and approvingly.

There followed a frenzy of activity in her bedroom upstairs as Miss Bethingame's own maid rushed to help her wash and change into a simple morning gown. There was also a turmoil in the young lady's mind. Why couldn't the Marquis of Carlyle simply be the overbearing, conceited Tulip she had imagined? Why did he have to have such a beguiling smile, such easy confidence? No, she told herself firmly, she was not going to fall for his well-practiced charm like every other girl in the neighbourhood. Let him play his games or whatever he was doing here, she had already told him that she had no wish to marry. In any event, he would soon tire of country ways and return to London, she was convinced, to seek his wife among the sophisticates there, leaving her to face her furious uncle. Well, at least he would not leave her with an aching heart!

Ferddie had returned to the drawing room to find Carleton pouring a glass of Madeira for Lady Burke, blithely recounting some tale of his aunt's pug. Milbrooke helped himself to another brandy and tried to catch his friend's eye, but the Marquis merely went on with his story. Ferddie shrugged and sat down—it was still Carleton's play—only to bounce up again when Miss Bethingame entered the room. This time she was charming in a plain muslin gown of light brown with orange ribbons, her hair simply caught back in a matching bow. Carleton took her hand and enquired about her headache, so Ferddie followed his lead with hopes that her good looks reflected her good health. Miss Bethingame coloured prettily, thanked her guests for their kindness and rang for tea before sitting down to discuss the gentlemen's ride over.

Lady Burke looked from Ferddie, nodding pleasantly, to Carleton, who was solemnly criticising the state of the roadways, to her perfectly lady-like niece, and told herself they were all candidates for Bedlam. She took another sip of her Madeira.

When the possibilities for conversation about the roads and the pleasant weather had been exhausted, Carleton addressed Lady Burke again, with the same degree of polite formality, to express an invitation to her and her niece, on behalf of his aunt Sephrina, Margaret's mother. There was to be another dance in honour of Margaret's engagement a sennight hence, a small, neighbourly affair, and Carle Manor would be honoured to host the Bethingame ladies. "Oh, yes," he concluded, "there will of course be card rooms for the nondancers in the party."

Elizabeth was undoubtedly going to refuse, Lady Burke knew, so she hastily accepted for them both. "How very kind of you. Elizabeth, dear, now you can wear the lovely lilac gown Ellie sent from London, can't you? Oh, my, how kind of your aunt, Lord Carleton." There was nothing for Elizabeth to do but acquiesce. She could not very well argue with her aunt in front of the gentlemen—her own ploy— nor could she express her opinion that Lord Carleton's aunt was so far unaware of the gracious invitation. She could only credit the Marquis's tactics, for whatever purpose he had in mind, knowing she had been skilfully manoeuvred into another function she would have declined and more of the public scrutiny she deplored. She could not help but distrust the smile Carleton was giving her; it was too calculating, too sure of success. Well, she might have to attend Margaret's party, but she did not have to dance with Margaret's cousin! Pointedly ignoring the Marquis, she turned to Ferddie Milbrooke, asking if he was also going to attend, which was a mistake on her part. Ferddie asked her for the first dance, as she knew he would, but Carleton had taken the opportunity for further conversation with Lady Burke. When Elizabeth could politely finish the talk with Milbrooke, it was to see Carleton as pleased as a cat full of cream and her aunt beaming.

"Elizabeth, you will never guess what a kind offer Lord Carleton has made! He has volunteered to teach you the waltz, to save us the bother and expense of hiring an instructor. Isn't that delightful? I think so, Elizabeth, for I am assured all the young ladies waltz now, although in my day... Well, I could not be more pleased, for to tell the truth I was meaning to talk to you about that very thing, Elizabeth. And, dear, I have invited Lord Carleton—and you, too, Lord Milbank—to tea tomorrow, for a lesson. Isn't that fine, dear?"

"That is Lord Mil*brooke*, Aunt Claudia, and, no, we have other plans for tomorrow afternoon, so we must regretfully decline my Lord's *kind* offer." Miss Bethingame was gritting her teeth over the polite phrases and glaring at her aunt. This was too much! Lady Burke, however, was never one for subtleties, especially when she saw her duties clearly and an object of desire in sight.

"Oh, do we have plans for tomorrow, dear? Well, then the following day, Lord Carleton, Lord Milbrooke? And perhaps we might have time for a round or two of whist."

Carleton agreed readily, and Milbrooke went along, so once again Miss Bethingame was trapped, committed to dancing lessons with a notorious flirt who only wished to embarrass her. "Thank you, I am delighted, to be sure."

Lady Burke was so pleased with the arrangements she believed she had made, and so thrilled at the interest Carleton was taking in her niece, that she thought to put the icing on the cake, so to speak: "Elizabeth, dear, why don't you show the gentlemen around the property? I am sure they would enjoy seeing the stables. All gentlemen do."

Elizabeth felt that she would gladly throttle her aunt, but to her surprise the Marquis declined, claiming they were overdue at Carlyle, and rose to leave. Ferddie naturally had to rise with him, though he was bewildered by his friend's decision to leave without seeing even one of the supposed champion stock. Why, he'd known Carleton to drive hours out of his way just to inspect a likely comer. Lady Burke was astonished that her trump card had failed. When her brother was alive, the place had simply thronged with gentlemen eager for such an invitation; since they were out of mourning, of course, the guests were much fewer, only a few close friends and childhood beaux of Elizabeth's, but none of them ever left without a survey of the new acquisitions. Even Miss Bethingame was thoroughly confused, especially after Carleton's casual, "Maybe next time." Only Carleton was satisfied as they made their farewells, though damn, he told himself, he would love a tour of the place!

# EIGHT

Two days later, as arranged, Carleton and Milbrooke rode over to Bething Manor for dancing lessons, tea and whist. Ferddie had been granted a higher degree of confidence and a better understanding of the role he was to play. In return, he had passed on, in exuberant adjectives, his impressions of the stables from his visit in the company of the spaniel and Jackson, the trainer and manager.

Equipped with sheet music, a meat pastry wrapped in paper to appease the pug and his friend's information, Lord Alexander Carleton was looking forward to the afternoon's curious diversions. Not so Miss Bethingame, who was presently in her bedroom, ransacking her wardrobe. She did not wish to give the Marquis a wrong impression by dressing to the hilt for him, as her aunt wished; neither did she want to appear ungainly before two London gentlemen come to teach the country bumpkin how to waltz. Miss Bethingame was not used to fussing with her appearance, nor worrying over others' opinions of her behaviour, and she was not enjoying this new experience. She almost convinced herself that she did not care what Carleton thought of her, yet the brown muslin was too plain, the pink silk too low-cut.... At last she decided on a burnt-peach gown edged at neckline and hem with ecru lace. It was not her most elegant or stylish day-dress, yet she thought it one of Ellie's most becoming, and she felt sorely in need of the confidence the gown could give her.

Too much time had been spent in the selection to leave much opportunity for leisurely dressing. Her brown-gold hair was quickly and skilfully coerced by Bessie, her maid, into a fashion known as Grecian curls, with a wisp or two of hair escaping to frame her face. Matching ribbon was provided, and her mother's pearls, her only jewelry. Perhaps it was the colour of the dress, or the hurry, or the nervous anticipation, but Miss Bethingame's colouring was at its finest, not the commonplace pink and white, but a lovely rosy glow. Again, perhaps it was Bessie's proud compliments or her own resolution to be on her guard, but the gold in Elizabeth's wide brown eyes sparkled with animation seldom seen in blue or green ones. Bessie smiled fondly. She'd told old Lord Bethingame what a beauty his daughter would be; it was a shame he could not be here to share it. Bessie also regretted for the thousandth time that her darling would not get to shine at a London Season . . . a motherless girl with a skinflint uncle and a balmy aunt. The maid shook her head. At least the fine gentlemen downstairs might appreciate her treasure. Better a Town buck than an old Lancashire widower!

The gentlemen were indeed appreciative, Ferddie with his charming compliments, Carleton with his beguiling smile. Then it was down to serious business, the Marquis taking charge. No more teasing or conniving; he was a strict taskmaster. Lady Burke fumbled at the pianoforte while Carleton turned the pages and marked the tempo. Milbrooke danced first with an ungraceful partner, twirling a gilt chair around the drawing room to give Elizabeth the idea. If anyone thought to question why Ferddie should do the dancing, Carleton the instructing, no one mentioned it. Miss Bethingame was half-relieved, half oddly disappointed, but the lesson proceeded smoothly. Her natural grace and sense of rhythm, coupled with the coordination developed through years of riding, stood her in good stead. She was never made to feel a clumsy fool, even when she miscounted her steps or Carleton criticised her inattention to the tempo. He was impersonal; Ferddie was patient. Together they commended her quick grasp of the dance, and in no time at all she was actually enjoying herself. Too soon Carleton called a halt, congratulating Lady Burke on her niece's aptitude:

"One more session for practice and she shall be as proficient as any lady at the dance, don't you think, Ferddie?"

"Lovelier, I'll wager."

Basking in such praise, Miss Bethingame could not be offended when arrangements were made for another lesson in two days' time. She was serving tea and conversing easily with Lord Milbrooke about the other guests to be expected at Margaret's affair, for he would be one of the few strangers present. Talk turned to some of the region's more colourful citizens, with Carleton and Miss Bethingame trading stories for Ferddie's amusement. The hour passed pleasantly enough, until a table was cleared for cards. Miss Bethingame admitted to a sad lack of skill at yet another art, but it was seen to be more from lack of interest than slowness of wit. She played a great deal better when sides were switched and Carleton was her partner, yet had to struggle to keep her concentration on the cards. Lady Burke made the gentlemen promise a return match when they declared it was time to leave, so she was well satisfied. Once again she invited her guests to visit the stables before leaving—this time with a degree of curiosity—and once again Carleton refused with some polite pretext. Miss Bethingame began to feel a prick of irritation, that his show of indifference might betoken disdain for the Folly's puny efforts. She did manage to thank him with genuine sincerity for his instruction, though, and Ferddie for his patience: "I do hope I did not scuff your boots too badly, Lord Milbrooke."

"Not at all, ma'am. It was my pleasure, I'm sure. You'll see, next time will be real dancing."

The next lesson began the same, Elizabeth and Ferddie waltzing while Carleton looked on, giving praise or blame to either indiscriminately. Lady Burke gamely played on.

A short interlude passed this way before the Marquis announced that now Miss Bethingame must waltz as a woman, not a schoolgirl. She must be able to relax, to carry on a conversation with her partner, not minding her feet or the count, or Ferddie may as well be dancing with the chair. Ferddie made her laugh at this, with his nonsensical description of the various styles of chairs he had partnered at debutante balls. Before she was aware of it, Miss Bethingame had overcome her first nervousness and found herself gliding without conscious effort, *feeling* the music while hearing and joining Ferddie's gay repartee.

The fun stopped when the Marquis laid his hand on Milbrooke's shoulder and quietly asked, "May I?" Miss Bethingame's insides gave a lurch, and a shiver twinged at her spine as he bowed before her. She returned an uncertain curtsey, surprised to see Ferddie changing places with her aunt at the piano bench.

"Now you must learn to waltz as it was meant to be danced," Carleton told her softly as Ferddie turned pages in the music book, "elegantly, romantically... seductively. The waltz was wickedly improper once, and you must dance the *why* of that." He spoke in a low voice, to her alone, as Ferddie began to play surprisingly—astonishingly—well. What embarrassment she might have felt at his words, what offense even, vanished as they began to dance. He held her closer than Ferddie had, more firmly, not letting her lower her eyes from his as the magnificence of Ferddie's music surrounded them. Carleton danced effortlessly; she could never be awkward in his arms. They swirled around furniture she was not aware of, and a part of her mind finally understood why the waltz was banned for so long in polite society.

"When you waltz," the Marquis was saying, "really waltz, you must look at your partner as though he were the only man whose arms you ever wished around you. He must look at you as... as I am."

The rest of the dance was a dream Elizabeth only awoke from at her aunt's applause. Elizabeth blushed furiously, then covered it by turning to Ferddie.

"Why, Lord Milbrooke, how marvelously you play! I had no idea!"

"Oh, I am out of practice now," he discredited the praise. "Don't get much opportunity, you know." Still, he beamed under their combined approval, especially the ladies' exclamations when Carleton told them what a rare treat they'd had, as Ferddie generally refused to play in public.

Tea was called for, with a discussion of music happily continuing. Ferddie turned out to be the most knowledgeable, though Carleton and Miss Bethingame found their tastes more similar. Lady Burke had to be apprised of the latest composers finding patrons among the London *ton*, pleased to agree with his criticism of the dilettante set though she had not the slightest understanding of his disdain.

A card table was again prepared, but three hands found Miss Bethingame guilty of her second bidding error.

"I am sorry, my Lords, Aunt Claudia; I simply do not have a head for cards!" she apologised. She really felt she needed some fresh air. "Perhaps if we conclude the game early this afternoon you might wish to visit the stables with me, if you are interested." She directed this last to Carleton, testing him, yet she was unsure what answer would have pleased her most.

He gave her that same beguiling, lopsided smile which

she was learning was half-irony, half-true amusement. "If *you* wish us to come, I would be honoured," he answered, reflecting her own uncertainty back at her and dismaying her by seeming to read her mind.

"I've seen the stables, Miss Bethingame," said Milbrooke. "Perhaps I'll just have a hand or two of piquet with Lady Burke, if that is all right with you, ma'am?"

Lady Burke was delighted, although she could not help feeling a trifle guilty over this lapse in chaperonage. Jackson would be there, however, and the entire stable crew, and it would only be a hand or two . . . .

Elizabeth led Lord Carleton down the rear hallway, and would have simply left the house but for the Marquis's reminder that she would need a wrap. He glanced at her teasingly, at her flimsy gown with its short, puffed sleeves. He knew she was disconcerted enough to forget the spring chill, and she knew that he knew, and was only more uncomfortable. Happy for the excuse, no matter how temporary, she asked him to wait in the nearby library while she fetched a shawl. She spent a few minutes in her room, arranging the shawl on her shoulders and trying to settle her thoughts. Was the Marquis trying to fix her attention or not, she wondered. She had so little experience with these matters she could not tell. He knew how she felt about surrendering the Folly to a stranger or allowing herself to be married off in some land transaction, so why was he flirting with her? Most likely because it was in his nature, she decided; but why, she asked herself furiously, must something in her respond to him?

The Marquis had been surprised at the library, at first. One long side of the large room was indeed stocked floor to ceiling with all manner of books, though whole shelves were reserved for horse-oriented volumes. The shelves on an adjoining side of the room held all sorts of trophies, cups, ribbons and certificates, attesting to Lord Bethingame's accomplishments. The other short side of the room held the large stone fireplace, with a superb jade horse on the mantle. T'ang Dynasty probably, Carleton thought approvingly. The same deep green was tastefully matched in the heavy brocade draperies, the worn leather of the chairs. The room was comfortable, masculine, familiar, except for the other long wall. This was hung with every odd size, shape and style of painting—all of horses! He was admiring some, chuckling over others, noting that each was by a different, unknown artist, when Miss Bethingame returned, much composed.

"Oh, you've discovered the family portrait gallery, have you?" she said with a laugh. "Papa always felt so sorry for the young artists hoping for a commission that he would let them paint his horses. Word got out, and every so often one would appear with a sad tale. Some of them had never painted a horse before, as you can see, but Papa was always willing to let them try and he, at least, was never disappointed."

Carleton laughed. "And did he never commission any to paint his daughter?"

"Oh, no, he felt it would be a waste until I grew up! I think he was afraid, also. You see, we do have one fine miniature upstairs. It is of my mother, but she took a fever shortly after it was completed and never recovered. I was about six at the time but remember Papa feeling the portrait was bad luck, although he cherished it greatly."

"And you have been alone since then?" he asked curiously.

"Alone? Why, no, Papa was here, and Bessie, and my old governess. And Aunt Claudia came, and of course I had all the horses. Come, I'll show you."

The stables were well built, airy and dry. The dirt underfoot was neatly swept, the straw in the stalls fresh and sweet-smelling. Carleton had time for a look around while Miss Bethingame greeted the rambunctious spaniel; a whole crew of young men smiled and tipped their hats to her before continuing their chores. There was no stinting *here*, Carleton noted. Horses were being led in and out for grooming and exercise. Some were mares brought in for foaling, Elizabeth explained, others boarders for breeding to the Bething stud. There was no uncertainty about Miss Bethingame now as she led Carleton to the end stall to view the stallion, Beth's Moonlight, a direct descendant of Darley's Arabian, through Eclipse. He was a huge animal, dark bay with black points, steady and intelligent looking. He came to the gate to have his muzzle stroked and wuffled until a piece of sugar was found.

"He is magnificent," Carleton agreed. "But why don't I know his name? He must have a formidable racing record, to base the stud on, but I cannot place him."

"No, he never raced. He came up lame at the Ascot trials." She told it simply, not revealing the death blow it had seemed to her father, who had sold off his acreage and everything he had to meet the purchase price. "But you would have won, wouldn't you, boy?" She turned back to Carleton again: "He would have, too. Everyone said so. They would have destroyed him right there, but Robbie convinced Papa he could stand to stud, even if he never raced again. And enough people had seen him at the trials to be interested in his offspring. His breeding helped, of course."

Carleton could not help marvelling, while she continued, at the chance Lord Bethingame must have taken, marvelling further at this beautiful girl with shining brown eyes talking of stud fees and consistently productive breedings. Most young ladies would blush just to hear the words. And knowledgeable? If he had thought her stable manager to be totally in charge here, he silently acknowledged the fault. Miss Bethingame knew more about the lineage and points of every horse in the stable—only possibly barring his and Ferddie's—than he ever hoped to, and he was considered an extremely proficient and learned horseman, if not an absolute Corinthian. He followed meekly behind the slip of a girl and her dog as she paused at various stalls, describing the mares to him.

"This is Princess," she said fondly, holding out an apple, "another of our thoroughbreds. This will be her last foaling, and then she will be retired. She's earned a rest." Elizabeth looked up at the Marquis happiy. "She is the Pride's dam."

"The Pride?" Carleton asked, not having seen any such horse.

"Folly's Pride, and our hope, too! He is from Princess and Moonlight, the match my father kept trying for and kept getting fillies! The Pride will take over the stud in a few years, after he has raced—and what a record he'll have! Robbie says he is better than Moonlight ever was and has stronger bones besides. We have him entered in the Ardsley Cup in a few months. Even a *good* showing will be enough, for his maiden race, to show everyone Papa was right. And if he wins, the price for Moonlight's service goes up, and the price of Princess's new foal! Oh, I wish you could see him," she said excitedly, all awkwardness between them forgotten for the moment. "Robbie has to keep him over by the cottage because it upsets Moonlight to have him nearby. We train him in the morning—we have our own practice oval; you can't see it from here. Perhaps some morning next week you would—" She caught herself, but it was too late. "That is, perhaps you might be interested in seeing him."

There was no chance for the Marquis to reply as Ferddie entered the stables with Lady Burke just then; there was no need, either, for his pleased smile was answer enough.

# NINE

The weather on the day of Margaret's second engagement party was not promising. Rain had fallen heavily the entire day and night preceding and was only now subsiding to a steady drizzle. The roads would be mired, difficult for horses and coach, uncomfortable for passengers. Fearing that her niece would use this as an excuse to stay home, Lady Burke kept herself out of Elizabeth's way. She did not come down to luncheon, sending a message that she wished to be well rested for the evening, and Elizabeth would do well to follow suit. She was relieved when her maid returned with a tray and a reply, merely Elizabeth's wishes for her undisturbed relaxation and the thought that perhaps they should be ready somewhat earlier than planned to allow extra time for the trip. Now Lady Burke's rest could indeed be peaceful; nor did she have qualms over meeting her niece at tea.

Elizabeth was totally resigned to attending the dance, with no intention of backing out. The thing she had dreaded most about the ball at Carlyle itself, being up for appraisal by some profligate son, had already occurred. The second worst thing which could have happened—and did—appearing backward over the waltz, was now resolved. Any resentment which might still linger was overshadowed by the promise of pleasure that the evening brought. She saw no reason why she could not simply enjoy herself as other girls her age did. She might have single-mindedly determined to remain unmarried for the Folly's sake, but she was learning to appreciate male company for her own! She was woman enough to take pride in the compliments, and girl enough to desire friendships among her own age group, something sadly lacking in her day-to-day life. If she would not admit to actual eagerness, at least she was not showing the defiant anger of a week ago, her aunt was pleased to see. Lady Burke was further reassured when Elizabeth dimpled prettily over the parcels just delivered from Carlyle Hall. One was a small nosegay of tiny wild violets, to match her lilac gown. The card simply read, "Yrs., Carleton." The second package was a satin-covered program book, with "As promised, F. Milbrooke" written in for the first dance. Lady Burke was too busy delightedly opening the third, a lovely orchid corsage with both gentlemen's compliments, to pay further attention to her niece. Elizabeth was turning the pages in the program and finding them curiously empty, as though Carleton was not going to ask her to dance. Perhaps the roads would be too treacherous for travel, after all, she thought.

The rains stopped, the sun broke through just long enough, and the ladies from Bething Manor arrived in good time. Lady Burke was swept off to the card room where earlier arrivals were waiting to make up a hand. Elizabeth was greeted warmly by Margaret with a kiss on the cheek, then drawn upstairs to freshen herself. Other young ladies were already there, laughing and gossiping happily. They hurried to Elizabeth, begging to know if rumours were true, if she really was on friendly terms with two such Nonpareils. Margaret laughed at her blushes and told the other girls not to tease. Elizabeth knew almost all of the young women, but none closely. They had attended each other's birthday parties at an earlier age, until most were sent off to be educated and only had school holidays in which to keep up with old friendships. Later they were all taken to London for their debutante balls and Seasons, widening the gap even further. Elizabeth had started out with them, even attending a fashionable seminary for young ladies, but she had missed her father terribly, and he was lonely without either his wife or his daughter, so she returned to be educated at home. Then came all the horses and more to interest the Bethingames at home than out visiting, and less money for entertaining, until Elizabeth hardly knew her childhood friends. She might have rekindled some old friendships when she reached the age of dances and parties, but her father's death and the year of mourning only isolated her more. She had found that she had very little in common with other young women her age when they did happen to meet—until tonight, when they were all exclaiming over each other's gowns and hair styles and beaux. She was delighted when her gown was complimented and gave Ellie's —Mademoiselle Elena's—direction to anyone who was interested with the highest recommendation. The gown itself would have been reference enough. Of pale lilac in a soft crepe, it had the same elegant simple lines which molded Elizabeth's figure so becomingly. The décolletage was daringly low, with Carleton's violet nosegay pinned at the V, lending a curious touch of innocence to the gown's sophistication. It was the envy of the other girls, all in beribboned, sequined confections. They glittered, but Elizabeth glowed! In fact, between her dress and the attention of the two most eligible bachelors in the neighbourhood, it seemed as though some old-time acquaintances would not develop into new-found friends. Others managed to hide their jealousy, hoping that some of Elizabeth's luck, as they called it, would rub off. One girl even asked if Elizabeth could introduce her to one beau or the other, for it was not fair for her to monopolise both! Miss Bethingame laughingly denied any rights of possession to either gentleman, gave a final pat to the curls piled luxuriously on the top of her head and descended the stairs with the rest.

Margaret's mother welcomed her kindly, telling Elizabeth that they must see more of her. Then there was Ferddie, waiting to claim her for the first dance. He looked marvelous in his evening clothes, putting all the local boys to shame trying to be fashionable with their ridiculously high shirt collars and glaring waistcoats. When Milbrooke told Miss Bethingame how enchanting she looked, she could only say, "And so do you!" which had them both smiling.

Margaret and Captain Hendricks took the floor and so the dance began. Elizabeth could not help glancing around to see if she could spot Carleton, but if he was present, he was not dancing. At the conclusion of the set, having bespoken the first dance after supper, Ferddie returned Elizabeth to her hostess, where Robert Carleton instantly asked her to stand up with him. She had vaguely known Robert all her life, too, so conversation was not difficult. He even recalled a visit to the Folly with his father once and remembered a tomboy in pigtails, to her embarrassment. She had a quick glimpse of blond curls atop a broad back— Margaret's partner—and had to have Robert repeat his question about the stables. Her next partner, also waiting at the hostess's side, was Captain Hendricks, so Elizabeth was able to congratulate him on his engagement and ask about plans for the wedding. She had the odd feeling that since this was such an informal party, the other girls were not being so strictly chaperoned, yet there was nothing she could say. Next came a country dance, with each successive partner only having a few minutes to introduce himself and utter a polite phrase. As Elizabeth turned to meet the next gentleman on her right in the rearranged figures, she looked up to see glittering blue eyes laughing down at her surprise.

If Ferddie's good looks put the other men to shame, Carleton made them look like farm hands, with his coat of blue superfine stretched across his broad shoulders, his white knee-breeches fitting just so, diamond stickpin accenting the gleaming white folds of his cravat. Even with

78

her limited experience, Elizabeth knew the Marquis would be outstanding in any crowd of men. His eyes were so blue, his nose so straight, his chin so strong—he could be dressed in rags and still hearts would flutter, hers for one.

The figures of the dance were changing; they had hardly exchanged "good evenings" when they separated, but Carleton did ask for the next dance.

He was waiting for her at the sidelines and made a low bow as the supper dance was announced. A girl's partner for this set was obliged to escort her through the buffet. Elizabeth wondered if the Marquis had known it would be this dance, remembering how just last week he had fled to the library rather than face it. He did not seem disconcerted by the announcement, and she could think of no graceful way to excuse him from the dance without leaving her to go to supper alone, so she merely smiled, returned a curtsy and allowed him to lead her to the floor.

"I must apologise, my Lord," she began, "I did not thank you for the lovely violets you sent."

"Didn't you?" he asked, looking at the nosegay nestled against her breasts, somehow making her feel the bouquet was the only thing she had on! As if he could sense her embarrassment, he went on in a different tone: "I hope you appreciate them fully. I had to go pick them myself, in the rain!"

"What, couldn't you send someone?"

"And have the whole estate know how romantic I was being? No, it would ruin my reputation!"

"Did you really go in the rain? It was unnecessary, I'm sure..."

"So am I, but it was worth it!" he answered. "Tell me, are you enjoying yourself?"

His tone was serious, as if he honestly cared. She had no hesitation in answering that yes, indeed, she was having one of the most pleasant evenings of her life. They sat with Ferddie and a Miss Faversham, a frothy blonde damsel who chattered through the meal. It did not pass anyone's notice that Lord Carleton and Miss Bethingame were on easy terms; they were a topic of interest which became a Thing as the Marquis led Elizabeth to his mother at the conclusion of supper. Luckily Miss Bethingame was unaware of the connotation of the honour, for she was able to converse with the Duchess unaffectedly. She was pleased at the likeness the Duchess saw in her to her mother, and proud when the Duchess noted that the Duke had always thought highly of her father. Whatever else Miss Bethingame might be, she was not shy and did not merely stand gawking at the exquisite beauty of Lady Carlyle, who was equally pleased that her old friend's daughter had turned out so charmingly. Somehow they had become the centre of a group of laughing young men—the Marquis had excused himself—and peculiarly enough, the Duchess nonchalantly undertook to sort them out and make introductions—the functions of a chaperone. Elizabeth was worrying over this when Millbrooke came for their second dance together.

"Oh, think nothing of it, Miss Bethingame; didn't she say she knew your mother? I am sure she won't mind all your beaux, especially with the Duke not present." Milbrooke laughed. "He said Carleton and I were all the escort any woman could want.... Incidentally, I'll be saying goodbye, leaving for London in the morning, you know."

"No, I hadn't known. I'm sorry to hear it; you've been so kind." She meant it, and Ferddie was touched. "I'll be seeing you shortly, at any rate."

"What a peculiar notion, Lord Milbrooke. How could you be seeing me? I do not go to London."

"No?" He looked a little confused. "Well, um, Carleton is staying on, so I shall likely be visiting again soon. I'm down often, you know."

Elizabeth gave an immediate invitation to call on his return, meanwhile wondering how much longer the Marquis was planning to remain in the country, away from all the entertainments of London. She also wondered if now, having had two dances with Milbrooke, she could expect

Carleton to ask her again also. He was not among the crowd around the Duchess, however, when Ferddie led her there without any hesitation after the dance. She was overwhelmed at first at the compliments waiting for her and the number of young men wishing to dance. The Duchess laughed at her confusion over the clamour, then kindly intervened.

"Come, my dear, you must get used to being the belle of the ball! Here, I'll decide. Mr. Rivington, you shall have the honour of this dance with Miss Bethingame, only because your father was a beau of mine."

After two or three partners, pleasant, friendly young men from the neighbourhood, were selected for her in such a fashion, Elizabeth began to feel a little uncomfortable. The other girls were chatting among themselves between dances, flirting with a few young men and accepting their own partners. The only explanation she could think of was the suspicion that she was to be kept busy—away from the Duchess's own son. But no, he was standing with a group at the other side of the room and had not even approached her, or the Duchess. Besides, her Grace was truly being kind; perhaps it was just her sense of propriety, knowing Elizabeth's aunt to be such a slipshod chaperone. Still, Miss Bethingame was uneasy, especially when the Duchess's manner underwent a change at the next introduction.

"Miss Bethingame, here is Sir Edwin Harkness, who swears his night would be ruined without a dance with you." Her voice was an icicle dripping disapproval. Elizabeth would have asked for an explanation, fearing she had committed some social blunder, but Sir Edwin made such a laughable picture in his exquisitely flourished bow that all her attention was drawn to him. Here was a true Tulip of fashion, and proud of it, right from his neckcloth, tied so high he could barely nod, to the rhinestone buckles on his shoes. In between was a checked velvet waistcoat crossed with enough fobs to keep an entire village from losing its timepieces! There were rings on every finger and lace dripping everywhere Elizabeth looked. She was amazed no, dumbfounded. She could only murmur slight appreciation as Sir Edwin began a strain of flattery as elaborate as his dress. Right there in front of the frowning Duchess and a handful of young men from the country, he likened her brown curls to the rivulets in a stream, flowing in the sunshine. Her skin became gardenia petals, her eyes those of a gentle doe. This was becoming ridiculous, she thought, comparing these inanities to Ferddie's sweet compliments, Carleton's smiles of approval. The music was beginning, and she heard snickers from James Rivington, for one; Miss Bethingame was growing embarrassed, indignant and in danger of losing her temper. "Sir Edwin," she began hurriedly when he had finished a description of her swan-like neck and was staring intently at the cleavage her gown revealed, "I am neither a dumb animal nor a babbling brook. Incidentally," she added mischievously, looking him straight in his watery blue eyes, "I am not an heiress either. Do you still wish to dance?"

It was Sir Edwin's turn to be embarrassed as he quickly led her to the dance floor to escape the laughter bubbling up around him and the bravos shouted for Elizabeth's wit. The Duchess looked across the floor to her son, who was glaring furiously, out of hearing. The Duchess smiled at him confidently. There was no need to worry about Miss Bethingame on *that* score; she was well able to take care of herself!

Nevertheless, Carleton was at the Duchess's side at the completion of the dance, when Elizabeth returned. He did not offer for the next set, though, nor the following, but only chatted amiably with the new beauty's admirers. Elizabeth could not help but note that most of the others were younger than Carleton and seemed more subdued in his presence. In fact, they no longer seemed so anxious to stand up with her! No one said one nice thing about her dimples or her turned-up nose! Perhaps Carleton sensed the effect he was having, for he soon wandered off, saying that perhaps now it was safe to meet the chit Robert was interested in.

The last dance was announced shortly, a waltz. Since this was a country ball where the guests had to travel some distance to get home, it would end much earlier than the grand London fêtes, which often went on till dawn. As Elizabeth sadly looked to the Duchess for her last partner, she told herself she was only regretting the last dance of her first real ball; she knew very well that she was disappointed not to have a last dance with the Marquis. She had hoped he was waiting for the waltz after making sure she would dance it this time, but he was not among those clamouring for the honour. The Duchess was talking to an older man, not aware of Elizabeth's difficulties. Where Elizabeth had almost resented having her partners chosen for her, she now realised what a relief it had been. She did not wish to slight anyone, but she was determined not to miss her very first waltz out in company. She was just about to select the nearest gentleman when a deep, mellow voice spoke at her back: "I believe this dance is mine, Miss Bethingame?" Elizabeth looked quickly over to the Duchess for any hint of disapproval, but Lady Carlyle nodded reassuringly, perhaps recalling the last dance of the week before. With a radiant smile, Elizabeth turned and almost floated into the Marquis's waiting arms.

If they had been a topic of interest before, they were now an established Fact, as far as anyone watching them dance was concerned. In truth, the only one not hearing wedding bells was Miss Bethingame herself, who was too happy to consider tomorrow!

# TEN

Tomorrow came quickly, before the dawn. In fact, it was waiting for Elizabeth at home in the form of an unannounced, uninvited visit from the present Earl of Bething, her Uncle Aubry. That gentleman had been conducting business in London, where some interesting tidbits of gossip had reached his ears. He had immediately altered his plans in order to pay a visit to his niece and sister. His usual communication was through the mails or solicitors, but this time he felt a personal call was in order to discuss some matters with his ward and to find out from his sister if there was any truth to the gossip. Luckily he was already asleep in a guest bedroom when Miss Bethingame arrived home so was saved from a rather terse, unlady-like but unmistakable expression of his ward's opinion of his arrival, right there in the front hallway.

"Elizabeth!" cried her aunt, hurrying her upstairs, away from the servants. "He is your uncle and your guardian!"

"Yes, and he was content to ignore my very existence here for two years until the Folly turned a profit. Never once has he offered to help us in any way, except to find fault!"

"But he did bring you the kind offer from that gentleman in Lancashire, remember?"

"Oh, yes, I remember. I remember how my value went up as soon as I reached breeding age! Do you recall how he threatened to cut off my allowance when I refused—an old man I had never seen and would have to give up my home and all I loved to marry. No, Uncle Aubry has never cared for *my* welfare, you can be sure of that. Just look around you; see all the things we need, and where is the money? *My* money. He refuses to give me any but an allowance till I am wed, he says. Well, I shall reach twenty-one before that day, and then we'll see."

"Oh, dear, you know it is no great sum of money. Your father simply did not have enough to leave you. He put it all into the horses, you know."

"I also know he meant for me to feed those horses without having to beg some solicitor for Uncle Aubry's consent. Uncle would only love me to fail so he could sell the Folly at a profit, just as he is trying to sell me!"

"Oh, Elizabeth," her aunt fretted, "you mustn't talk like that. You know what Aubry thinks of free-spoken females. I'm sure that if you are pleasant to him and show a little respect, he will be more understanding. Do try not to get so riled up; you know how these scenes are so disturbing to everyone."

Elizabeth did know, indeed. Her uncle's last visit—with his clear intention of seeing her engaged to his widower friend—had gone so badly poor Aunt Claudia had had a headache for three days. This time, Elizabeth vowed as she undressed in her own room, she would prove to her uncle that she was a mature woman, able to conduct her own affairs in a rational, unemotional manner. There would be no raised voices or accusations this time, she swore to herself, only steadfast logic—and a desire to see him gone. She unpinned the violets from her gown and set them in a glass of water next to her bed. With Uncle Aubry settled in her mind, she was able to go to sleep thinking of pleasanter thoughts, like laughing blue eyes.

When she awoke in the morning, later than usual, the violets were drooping miserably, but Elizabeth's determination to impress Uncle Aubry with her poise still held firm.

She called for Bessie and hurriedly dressed in a demure muslin morning gown, then went to the breakfast room, instead of to the stables first, which was her usual custom. Her aunt was dressed and down, also out of the ordinary, for Lady Burke seldom left her rooms before noon, preferring not to know how her niece spent the time. Today, however, she felt her presence was necessary, little though she enjoyed being the buffer between these two rock-hard temperaments, having learnt from experience that is was the soft buffer who inevitably suffered.

Elizabeth greeted her uncle surprisingly cordially, and enquired of him about her aunt, a devout, disapproving lady, and her dear young cousins, a pack of runny-nosed brats. She even asked about Bething, the family seat, a ramshackle old mansion Elizabeth had had to visit with her father once a year. Uncle Aubry had always lived there, managing the property for his brother even before he came into the title. Elizabeth's father had bought the Folly property before his marriage, knowing the dreary northern estate was no place for his lovely bride, nor the grim spinster aunts and retired soldier uncles suitable companions. Aubry and his wife had never minded the whole flock living there until, of course, they had to pay the bills themselves. By now most of the old relations were passed away and Bething was simply a moldering, drafty old building, which only Uncle Aubry could take pride in claiming. His pride was enormous, even more so now that he was its rightful, titled owner, not just its steward. He expounded all through breakfast over crops and tenants and structural improvements. Elizabeth and her aunt listened attentively until he digressed to his neighbours, one Lord Cedric Barnable in particular. Having heard enough about Lord Barnable on her brother's last visit, Lady Burke was sure this was not a safe topic for conversation. She quickly interrupted:

"Forgive me, dear Aubry, but I have to ask how long you will be visiting with us; our pleasure, of course, but

Cook must be told so we might be sure of having things just as you like them."

Elizabeth was toying with the fringes of resentment. It had not escaped her notice that Uncle Aubry had not asked about *their* welfare or the improvements being made here. Though she was determined to be polite, she felt her aunt was going too far in trying to appease him, in making him feel actually welcome. She only hoped he would say whatever unpleasantness he had come for and leave this morning.

"Four or five days, I think," was her uncle's unfortunate reply, at which Elizabeth excused herself to some business at the stables to mask her disappointment. Before she reached the door, however, he stopped her with a summons to meet in the library in an hour's time. Elizabeth did not like his tone of voice, nor his peremptory orders to her in her own home. She merely nodded, figuring to get this over quickly so perhaps he would leave earlier, without making an issue of it.

Her business in the stables consisted mainly of sending a groom with a hurriedly written note to Carlyle Hall, requesting that Lord Carleton not call at Bething's Folly this week as was planned due to unfortunate circumstances. She regretted having to send the message—though a meeting between the Marquis and Uncle Aubry could only be trouble—and the regret simmered in the back of her mind as another black mark against her uncle. The looks of commiseration she received from the stable hands did not help at all, nor the "Lovely morning, Miss Bitsy" greeting from Jackson. It *was* a fine morning, clear and crisp after all the rain, but she was not to enjoy the freshness of the sunshine. No, she would be kept in like a child with lessons to hear some odious lecture.

Her uncle, meanwhile, was using the time to gather information. The talk in London was of some brown-haired Unknown capturing Carleton's fancy at a ball in the country last week. The house guests had returned from Carlyle Hall full of the tale, but not the young lady's name. She was said to be slight and quite good looking, if in an Original way, with a style all her own. Having been notified by his sister of the ladies' invitation to attend the ball, he dared let himself consider that for once his niece might have accomplished something worthwhile. Their very presence at another Carleton do last night reinforced his hopeful interpretation of the London gossip. Claudia was only too happy to satisfy his curiosity as long as it got Lord Barnable off his mind. She couldn't see the harm in expressing her own hopes as far as the Marquis was concerned, such a nice young man who even brought treats for her dog. She told about the dancing lessons and the violets, but she was unable to relate details of the dance last night, as she had been in the card rooms all evening. This brought censure down on her own head, for her deplorable gambling habits and her lackadaisical supervision of Elizabeth.

"Take my word for it, Claudia, she will shame us all some day with her hoydenish behaviour. There'll be a scandal sooner or later, unless there's a firm hand to control her."

"But perhaps some men prefer um . . . interesting women, Aubry." Lady Burke was twisting her napkin, worrying which of the servants knew of Carleton's first, disastrous visit, or how long he was alone in the stables with Elizabeth. Lady Burke did not think either occasion would make an outright scandal, but there was no underestimating her brother's sense of propriety, nor his pride in the Bethingame name.

"No man likes a flighty woman, Claudia."

"But Lord Carleton seems to be paying a deal of attention to her . . . ."

"And if the young fool can be made to offer for her soon, we'll be well out of it."

"But . . . but, Aubry, Elizabeth does not *wish* to be married."

"Rubbish, madam! What else is there for a woman to do?"

When Elizabeth returned to the library, it was to find her uncle sitting at her father's desk—now hers—going through her account books.

"Uncle Aubry! Those are my personal business!" she exclaimed, slamming one shut in front of him, furious at his intrusion but determined to stay calm.

"Nonsense, I am your guardian."

"And this is my house, as you very well know, to which you have not been invited."

"I do not *have* to be invited to attend to my ward's business." Lord Bethingame saw no fault in his own actions, merely another instance of his niece's waywardness. He chose to ignore her insulting manner and gestured her to a seat.

She threw herself into a leather chair and immediately began tapping her foot. "What, pray tell, is this business you have suddenly concerned yourself about?" she asked. "I have told you I will not marry any of your old cronies, so you may as well give up on that."

"This has nothing to do with your wedding anyone; I doubt if any of my friends would have you! That is beside the point.... Claudia wrote me about a horse you are entering in the Ardsley Cup races this season."

"That is correct. We have great hopes for him."

"It won't do."

"What do you mean, it won't do? He is a fine horse and stands a great chance." She was genuinely puzzled.

"It won't do because horse racing is not a proper vocation for respectable young women."

"That is absurd. Lady Jeffreys runs her own stables, and Lady—"

"Lady Jeffreys has been through three husbands, which is not exactly respectable, but that is entirely irrelevant. Neither Lady Bethingame nor myself approves of horse racing, especially for women. We do not wish our name associated with such a debacle."

"Uncle Aubry, neither Aunt Eunice nor yourself have

ever approved of anything I did, or my father before me, so that is not a prime consideration. What is is that this horse can prove our stud. He can win the Cup, the money, the honour. I have a fine trainer in Robbie Jackson, and an experienced jockey. There will be no disgrace."

"Nevertheless, he will not run."

"Not run? Of course he will! Haven't you been listening? He is entered; he can win."

"Your horse has been withdrawn. That is what I was doing in London, speaking to the stewards of the race."

"What?" Elizabeth was on her feet in front of the desk, shouting. "You can't do that! You have no right!"

"You are under age, Elizabeth. It is my right, no, my duty, to protect your reputation. The stewards will not accept your horse without your guardian's consent. I will not give it. I have also made clear to the officials that if your horse runs under another's name, they had better have ownership papers to prove it."

Elizabeth was in a rage. If the Pride did not race, the Folly could not get by much longer on Moonlight's reputation. If the Pride were sold, then raced, they would have the reputation, but no stallion in a few years. Either way the Folly would be finished. Tears of rage filled her eyes until, instead of seeing the thin, balding man in drab clothes in front of her, she saw all the injustices of her life; instead of his pontifical voice, she heard every condemnation of everything she loved. It was too much. Her hands, clenched into useless fists, pounded on the desk as she told her uncle exactly what she thought of him. An inkpot bounced on the desk at "despicable," she unconsciously grabbed it at "pompous," and when she brought her fist down, bottle and all, at "ass," the contents spewed all over her uncle.

And that was how Miss Elizabeth Bethingame conducted herself in a mature, reasonable manner.

When she left the house a short while later in a tossed-together riding outfit, she informed Taylor that her uncle would be leaving, to see that his bags were packed and his carriage brought round. She didn't know if she could carry it off, but Taylor, at least, saw no reason to disbelieve her and moved off to give instructions.

When Elizabeth returned home after some few hours, she was dust-covered and disheveled but not one bit more relaxed. Taylor informed her, with no hint of emotion or expression, that there must have been a misunderstanding; her uncle was departing in the morning, to avoid the discomfort of a night at an inn.

"The expense, you mean. Well, I shall have luncheon in my room and be out for tea.... Tell Cook to burn the dinner."

"Yes, ma'am. Begging your pardon, Miss Elizabeth, but a note was delivered to you this morning. I sent it up to your bedroom, in case, ahem, you should come in the rear door."

What he meant, Elizabeth knew, was that Uncle Aubry had been snooping around and the note was something she would rather he not see, or, at any rate, something Taylor thought was private. She smiled and ran up the stairs.

The note was on heavy bond, with a blue seal, and read: *Has your success of last night gone to your head already that you can dismiss old admirers? Yrs., Carleton.* She tore it into the smallest pieces the thick paper would allow.

No one saw Lord Bethingame off in the morning except Taylor. Lady Burke sent word that she was not feeling well; her headache would most likely last a week this time. Elizabeth had no intention of making even the slightest pretense at cordiality, so stayed in her rooms all morning pacing until Bessie finally brought word that he was gone. Elizabeth spent another hour in the library, composing letters to her solicitors to see what was to be done about that race. She could think of many plans—most impractical, some illegal, none satisfactory—but it was Robbie Jackson's suggestion that she make enquiries first to see if Uncle Aubry was only trying to cow her, or possibly overstepping his authority. The letters were sent off to catch the mail coach and Elizabeth picked at her solitary luncheon. She wasn't in the mood to ride, or watch the training exercises, or read, or anything—except maybe kick at a few doors. At last she tossed a shawl over her shoulders, called for her dog at the stables and set off on an aimless walk. She wandered down a way on the dirt lane while the spaniel chased imaginary rabbits, then around some of the paddocks, then finally back to the gardens, where she sank down on a marble bench. One hand idly stroked the dog behind his ears, but her thoughts were hundreds of miles away at a certain race track. She could see the horses running, hear the crowds shouting for the Pride, hear the officials calling her name....

"Miss Bethingame? Miss Bethingame?"

She jerked back to the here and now where, standing in the sunshine, tapping his riding crop against his boots, Alexander Carleton was concernedly looking down at her.

"Oh. Good afternoon, my Lord. I didn't see you approach." She gave him a vague smile.

"I know. I've been walking over all the place looking for you. Do you always go out without telling anyone where you are?"

"I was just thinking. Besides, I was not expecting anyone." She looked up at him suspiciously. "I believe I did ask you not to call."

"Yes, but I thought I might be of assistance." He did not say that he almost rode over as soon as he received her note to find out what had happened, what he could do to help. Instead he had sent a man with a nonsense reply, on a reconnaissance mission. The groom was not to return until he knew exactly what was going on at Bething's Folly. Carleton therefore knew all about her uncle's arrival, and more, but this was going to be one of those conversations where he had to proceed carefully, as were most with Miss Bethingame. She might speak her own mind with sometimes lamentable consequences; he dared not. For instance, while he wanted to take this forlorn little figure in his arms and comfort her, he teasingly asked if he might sit down, since she had neglected to invite him. As expected, she recovered enough spirit to advise him not to be a ninny. He was here, wasn't he? She made room for him on the marble bench; he chuckled and sat down, then asked if he might know what had caused her such distress.

"Ah, Sir Galahad. My uncle, that's what. An odious, obnoxious man. He arrived the night of Margaret's ball, all puffed up with his own righteousness, poking and prying into my business. He is refusing to let the Pride race in the Ardsley Cup because it would be a poor reflection on the family name! Have you ever heard such nonsense?"

"And what did you do?"

"Me? I ... I lost my temper."

"You, Miss Bethingame?" She looked over quickly and yes, there was that damnable smile. She had to smile back, her anger and despair forgotten for a moment. She even had to laugh when she described last night's dinner, the look on her uncle's face. She'd come down late, in a gown she had never worn because it was too low-cut, no matter how fashionable Ellie said it was. Then she had proceeded to feed her over-cooked quail to Aunt Claudia's pug, at which Uncle Aubry naturally took exception and ordered the dog removed. Elizabeth just as naturally declared it was *her* home and the dog would stay. None of the servants would interfere, suddenly disappearing into the kitchen. Claudia was wailing Oh my's into her napkin and Aubry, to prove his point and his power, made to evict the animal himself. With a stranger at his hindquarters and roast quail at his pushed-in nose, the dog's reaction was immediate— and painful to Lord Bethingame. Not too bloody, because of the old dog's rotten teeth, but enough.

"Uncle was almost apoplectic!" Elizabeth laughed. "You should have seen him!"

"I'm afraid I did...."

"What do you mean? He left early this morning, so you could not have passed him on the road."

"No, he—um—he stopped to pay his respects to the Duke on his way to London."

"But he doesn't even know the Duke, to my knowledge, and Carlyle is not on the way to London. I don't understand."

"Luckily the Duke was off with his bailiff; I had the, ah, pleasure of receiving your uncle." He went on quickly, before she could interrupt: "He mentioned you might be going to stay up north with him and his lady shortly."

"That's absurd! Aunt Eunice would never have me, even if I would go. No, whatever the purpose of his call, it was not that. I wonder what he really had in mind."

"I believe," Carleton said slowly, carefully, "that he wished to ascertain if my intentions toward you were honourable."

"Why, of all the encroaching, insulting—I hope you threw him out!"

"I did better than that. . . . I offered for you."

"You did *what?*"

"I asked his permission to make my addresses to you. Miss Beth—Elizabeth, please listen. I know this sounds horrible, and you have every reason to be angry. Since I hardly know you, only for a week or so, I have no right to speak of emotions; indeed, I'm sure you would only be offended. But if you consider this reasonably—don't look at me like that—you'll see the advantages of such a proposition. Think of it as a business transaction if you must. You will get to keep the Folly forever, with no guardians or overseers; your solicitors can draw up a contract so that neither the property nor the proceeds ever come to me or my family. You can leave it to your children, or charity! I promise never to interfere. You will, of course, have a marriage settlement to ensure your future and to refurbish the house, and you will still have your freedom to do whatever you want. We would have to take a house in London, of course, and spend some time there, but not too much. And we could live here, if you like, when we're in the country, instead of at Carlyle."

She was staring at him peculiarly, as if he had just sprouted another nose. "Excuse me, Lord Carleton—"

"Alexander, please."

"Lord Carleton. Sir, I wonder about your sanity."

He smiled but went on anyway. "I am entirely sane and serious. You already have my respect; I think we could learn to deal very well together."

"Lord Carleton, I do not wish to seem ungrateful of the honour, but you offer me my farm, my freedom, respect—and money, too. Exactly what do *you* get out of this, besides a wife you don't want?"

He knew this question would be coming, so he'd prepared an answer on his way over. He was not about to reply that he would get what he wanted most, the chance to hold her, to look after her, to teach her to love him as he loved her. No, he was sure enough of his stratagems but not confident enough to chance being repulsed by some independent young chit. He laughed at himself—his first offer of marriage, and the first woman he'd had to bargain with! Still, Elizabeth was waiting for an answer.

"I need a wife, you know that. I think you are someone whose company I could enjoy, who would understand my having interests of my own, as you have yours. You would be a wife I could be proud of, for make no mistake, there will be demands on you. You will be Duchess someday, remember. You will have to be presented and take your place in Society, run a household and entertain."

She was not satisfied, he could see that, but there was no more explanation coming. She asked, testing, "Could I race my horses under my own name?"

"Your name would be Carleton, of course, something I would have to insist on, but I would be pleased to have you use it if your horses are as good as you say. No one can stop you from keeping and using your stable's name, however, not even your uncle, though I would like to see him try."

"And the Ardsley Cup?"

"Yes, that's a problem, that and your uncle's threat to carry you away. I would have waited until we knew each other better, but the race is in two months and I know how much you are counting on it. I'm sure I've given you better reasons for accepting me, Elizabeth, but here is the most pressing: Your uncle simply won't let you race; I will.... Lord, I feel as though I'm proposing to a horse!" He laughed, sure she would see the ridiculousness of the situation as he did, or at least become angry, which would be equally in keeping. She remained very quiet, however, withdrawn, only saying she would need some time to consider what he had said.

Elizabeth remained in the garden for a long time after Carleton left, staring at nothing. She had just been offered two things she dearly loved—the Folly and, yes, Lord Alexander Carleton himself. Only one thing was missing, she thought bitterly. He'd spoken of respect and pride and contracts, not one word of love! He had not even kissed the woman he would marry. Tears streamed down her cheeks as Elizabeth cried for the first time since her father's death.

# ELEVEN

Things looked different to Elizabeth the next morning. Carleton mightn't love her, but he was willing to marry her, and that was a start! She could not refuse him, not for practical considerations, not for *any* reasons. When he came to tea her hand only trembled slightly as she poured for him and Aunt Claudia; her voice only quavered a little when she made the announcement: "Aunt Claudia, I have some news. Lord Carleton has done me the honour of asking me to be his wife, and I have accepted." Lady Burke's sweet roll dropped out of her fingers—the pug lunged for it. Her eyes filled with tears, the older woman jumped up to kiss Elizabeth, blubbering how happy she was. She offered her cheek to Carleton before rushing from the room to fetch Taylor and some champagne. When she had left, the Marquis raised Elizabeth's hand and kissed it.

"Thank you, Elizabeth. You'll see, it was the right choice." It was the only choice, as they both knew, but he was bound to show her every consideration.

There were champagne toasts and congratulations from Taylor and Cook and Bessie, and Jackson brought in, and exclamations over the heirloom diamond and sapphire ring presented for inspection, which was too big.

"I knew it wouldn't fit, but I wanted you to see it first. I could have it reset if you'd like, or buy a new one, if you would prefer," Carleton said when they were alone again.

"No, it is exquisite.... Did you know I'd accept, that you brought it along?"

He smiled. "I was hoping. Besides, it will save time. There's a great deal to be done. I shall be off to London tomorrow, now that that is settled. I wish to speak to your uncle before he leaves, have the house opened, make arrangements—all kinds of things. Come, walk outside with me, will you? We have a lot of details to consider."

The first problem was when to hold the wedding and where.

"Must it be a big wedding at St. George's in Hanover Square, with half the *ton*? I would much rather be married by the vicar here in the chapel, if that is agreeable to you," she said.

"That would be fine. I deplore those London circuses, and all the relatives we would have to have. It will mean a few less tablecloths and tea sets, but I dare say we'll manage without. Mother can be persuaded to hold a reception in Town, so no one will be too much offended. St. George's would take a great deal of time to arrange besides, I'm sure, so this will be better. My father's groom informs me that entries for major horse races are closed a month before the race date, which does not give us much leeway, if Elizabeth Bethingame Carleton is to appear on the papers. Do you like the sound of it?" He stopped walking to look down at her, but she chose to misinterpret his question.

"Then we must be wed shortly. Yes, that sounds fine. I can wear Mama's wedding gown, so I'll be ready whenever you obtain the license." She was trying not to bounce up and down in eagerness; he was disturbed by her lack of enthusiasm. They really did not know each other well. He took her arm and started walking again.

"No, we cannot simply be married like that. There will be gossip enough as is." Lord, he thought, if he just married her out of hand next week, what a feast the vultures would have on her reputation! "Besides, you should have a gown of your own, a trousseau and all those things. Why,

Margaret has started already, and she won't be married until next winter. You know, that just might help us. Mother has promised to take Margaret to London for her bride clothes. Perhaps they could be persuaded to go next week, and you and your aunt could be Mother's guests at Carlyle House. That way you can get introduced around before the announcement, see about your clothes, be there to look at houses with me."

"I don't know... Aunt Claudia won't travel. She says it makes her sick, but I believe it's the pug who can't stand long carriage rides. Either way she'll never go to London, just for a shopping expedition."

"Well, Mother will be happy to have you anyway; in fact, she could say you are a friend of Margaret's, so you won't be bothered so much at first." Details of the trip were left pending consultation with the Duchess. Other items were discussed, such as a companion for her aunt, the wedding breakfast, the honeymoon. They agreed the breakfast would be better held at Carlyle Hall, with its larger facilities. As to the wedding trip, Elizabeth refused to miss the last of her horse's training or the race itself, so they would return to London after the wedding to their new house, and plan a tour for the summer. This took care of immediate concerns, except for a letter to Elizabeth's solicitors concerning the legal contract to be drawn. Carleton wished to stop for it on his way to London in the morning.

"I never want you to think I married you for your property." He smiled, despite being serious. When he sensed she would have made some comment about why he *did* propose to marry her, he quickly went on: "I am sure my mother will want to call. May I bring her along when I come tomorrow morning?"

"Must she know about the contract, business transaction, as you call it?"

"She will only know that I offered for you and you did me the honour of accepting. She'll be thrilled. You're not sorry you did accept me, are you, because of all these details?" He smiled down at her, then gently put his hand to her cheek and lightly, quickly, kissed her. No, she was not sorry.

Elizabeth was a little nervous about receiving the Duchess, whose first words, however, after greetings and congratulations were "What can I do to help?" She expressed her delight in introducing Elizabeth to London, her readiness to agree to any plans Elizabeth and Carleton had already made. She regretted the haste in preparations but seemed to understand the difficulties about uncles and race horses as though they were an everyday problem. There were no experienced opinions being dictated to Elizabeth, no lectures about what she must do and not do. Seeing the two women so happily in sympathy with each other, and Aunt Claudia fussing contentedly, Carleton excused himself to continue his journey to Town with letters to the solicitors, Ellie and Elizabeth's old governess. He would return in a few days with, it was hoped, arrangements well under way, and then escort the ladies back to London when they were ready.

"Maybe I shall even get to see Folly's Pride between times," he joked on his way out. "Perhaps I'll ask him to be my best man."

After his departure, talk reverted to members of the wedding. Ferddie Milbrooke would of course stand up with Carleton; whom did Elizabeth have in mind for her attendants?

"I thought I might ask Margaret, your Grace, since I really have no one closer and we are to be cousins. There is a difficulty about someone to give my away, however," Elizabeth said uncertainly.

"I thought your uncle was your guardian...?"

"Yes, your Grace, he is, but I have never been *his*, to give away or not. In fact, I dislike him excessively and have refused to have him under my roof!"

"Oh, my. Alexander did warn me you were something of an Original." She said this with a smile, no hint of reproof. "Who else is there? No brothers, but a cousin perhaps? An uncle from your mother's family?"

"No, there is no one like that. I would love to have Robbie, who has been like an uncle to me, but I don't suppose it would do the Duke's health much good to have his daughter-in-law being given away by the head groom!"

Both women laughed, then the Duchess said, "Thank you for considering the Duke's feelings, my dear. I'm afraid my husband would find the idea enchanting, but I am afraid you would suffer when the newspapers recounted the tale. How would it be if your uncle were invited to Carlyle for the wedding? That way you would only need see him for the ceremony, not under your roof! You could say the house was filled, as I understand you'll want your governess here, and your Mademoiselle Elena, to help with your clothes."

"Yes, and we'll be having rooms redone for Lord Carleton," Aunt Claudia put in, surprising Elizabeth, who hadn't yet thought of that necessity.

"Of course. Are you sure you won't mind, your Grace, for there is my Aunt Eunice, too. She is nearly as impossible as Uncle Aubry."

"I assure you there is room enough at Carlyle Hall to lose an entire family tree of odious relatives! Are there children, too?"

"There are four terrible brats. I see no reason to invite them, especially with the chapel so small."

"What a shame. Flower girls and ring-bearers always look so charming."

"The girls would only trip each other in the aisles, your Grace, and one of the boys would be bound to swallow the ring!"

When even Aunt Claudia admitted that the stable boys would add more dignity to the occasion, the Duchess laughingly conceded. She went away from the visit well pleased and passed along her satisfaction to the Duke, together with an invitation for them to dine at Bething after Carleton's return, "If your Grace is up to it," the Duchess repeated, her eyes twinkling. "Oh, yes, your new daughter says that you might come early, if you wish to view the finest thoroughbred ever born to race."

" 'The finest thoroughbred ever,' is it? Yes, she's Bething's daughter, all right! Damn, I like the chit already. Well, tell her I am up to it!"

A flurry of activity now swirled around Elizabeth such as she had never seen in her quiet life. First there were preparations for her journey to London—she had to look her best to go shopping—a dinner for the Duke, renovation of certain rooms in the manor. There were letters, interviews and lists. Everything in the house had to be discussed with Taylor and Aunt Claudia, everything on the grounds with Jackson. When Carleton returned, he had great news of a small house on Grosvenor Square he was hoping she would approve. He also told her she might now go ahead with whatever plans she had for the Folly, as her own modest funds were finally released to her, plus a handsome marriage settlement. In addition, he had somehow managed to convince Uncle Aubry to pay for her trousseau, whatever she needed.

"So you can shop London bare! I expect to have the best-dressed wife in Town. Remember to order what you will need for the summer, too. Aubry expected a honeymoon trip."

"How did you do it? I can't imagine him offering such a gift!"

"Not without a little prompting. All it took was *my* offering to pay for your bride clothes. It didn't take him long to see how he would look if the bills for his ward were sent to me. So you have a special account just to handle your purchases."

Elizabeth clapped and was delighted to learn that her

uncle would already have left for his home by the time she reached London.

Dinner for the Duke and Duchess went smoothly, especially after Folly's Pride was brought up and paraded around the front drive. Carleton was still a little skeptical, saying he would like to see the beast run before he put money on him, but the Duke declared his prospects excellent, more so after Elizabeth recounted his background over dinner. The Duke could not have been more enthusiastically approving—of the horse and his son's fiancée—if he had raised them himself. He was so pleased with Elizabeth, in fact, that he told Carleton the Grosvenor Square house would be their wedding present, if she liked it, of course.

And then London! The trip alone was a novelty, with Margaret companionably excited. Elizabeth had been to Town with her father to see the sights and visit horse sales, but not since his death, not as a young woman. The crowds, the noise, even the dirt fascinated her all over again. Now she noticed gowns, carriages, houses. Mademoiselle Elena was sent for as soon as the ladies arrived in Berkeley Square. Ellie, all hugs and smiles, arrived with a carriage full of samples, sketches and assistants. The samples were discussed in committee first, for immediate needs. As Mademoiselle explained to the Duchess, the samples were always in Miss Bitsy's size, as repayment of the debt she owed the previous Lord Bethingame. She was as excited as Elizabeth that the new Earl would be paying for the new gowns, since she was not in his debt at all! Next, sketches were brought out, and swatches of materials. Ellie's design for the wedding gown was instantly approved, although laces could not be selected until the veil worn by generations of Carlyle brides was unearthed. Elizabeth ordered one special ball gown for utmost priority, the dinner-dance the Duchess would give in a week's time to announce the betrothal. She also chose designs for two other evening dresses, a military-style riding habit, and a promenade gown for now, summer gowns for later.

"Ah, *ma cherie*, there is no time for more! After the wedding, anything! Until then, this is all I can provide. You must patronise the other modistes also, it is only fitting for the wife of a Marquis."

Margaret was to have two of the sample gowns altered to fit since their colours were more becoming to her than to Elizabeth, and the Duchess ordered a gown from one of the sketches she admired, to be made up whenever it would be convenient. Deeply gratified, Ellie was certain that for the Duchess, next week would be convenient if she had to sew Elizabeth's wedding gown herself on the way to the ceremony!

The following days were spent shopping, indeed patronising almost every fashionable store in London. There were underclothes and nightdresses, shoes and bonnets to be purchased, in addition to more dresses for every imaginable purpose. Hours were spent in fittings and browsing, one entire morning at the Pantheon Bazaar selecting ribbons, fans and gloves. The Duchess often sent the two girls out with Bessie and footmen while she made social calls. After luncheon tradesmen came to show samples of wallpaper and upholstery fabrics for the Grosvenor Square House, which Elizabeth had loved at first sight. It even had a small garden in the back. Carleton was staying in his bachelor rooms, coming to Carlyle House for meals and these conferences. He generally approved Elizabeth's choices, except for his study, where he wished to place the furniture from his present residence.

"But I intend to use the study, too," Elizabeth protested. "In fact, I plan to do a lot of business while I am in London. I cannot discuss stud fees in a gilt-edged drawing room!" A compromise was reached whereby an office was created between the dining room and the present study, necessitating tearing walls down, more workmen, more confusion, but Elizabeth was satisfied. Carleton's days were mostly spent at the new house, overseeing the crews, or at various official buildings, tracking down permits and licenses. The two were almost never alone together, their only quiet times the short carriage rides in the park with Margaret along. Both girls had to be present for tea, for the Duchess was carefully inviting the most influential of London's hostesses to meet them. The Duchess never warned Elizabeth, "Lady Jersey comes today, so be on your best behaviour if you wish the voucher for Almack's," or "Lady Rothingill joins us; she is the worst gossip in Town." Elizabeth was introduced as a young friend of Margaret's, from the country. Although most of the guests had their own thoughts on the matter, such was the Duchess's stature that if she had declared Miss Bethingame a Red Indian princess from the colonies, so she would have been considered. It was the Duchess's game; she had only to announce the rules and everyone was delighted to play. Most of these women were impressed with Elizabeth for her own sake, as Lady Carlyle had counted on. Her natural charm was found to be unspoiled by the boredom affected among the sophisticates; neither was she awkwardly shy, like an unfledged debutante. Anyone who had known her mother was instantly her friend, as was anyone remotely interested in horses, fashions or a hundred other topics.

"What a refreshing change to find a girl with conversation," the Duchess was complimented, and "How fortunate for your niece to have such a lively, attractive companion." The voucher to Almack's was sent round the next day, and invitations began to pour in. Acceptances for the Duchess's own party were also forthcoming, keeping everyone busy with correspondence and lists in their free time, of which there was not much, especially since the Duchess insisted they all rest before dinner each day. Elizabeth and Margaret protested at first, but after a full day of being fashionable and a night at the theatre or the opera, they learned to welcome the respite. The Duchess was not accepting invitations this week, knowing there would be ample later, after Elizabeth's presentation at Court, her bow at Almack's, the engagement announcement. It was enough to let her be seen and enjoy herself before she became a curiosity. Carleton escorted the ladies, and Captain Hendricks when he could, and some gentlemen friends of consequence of the Duke and Duchess. Ferddie Milbrooke joined their number, too, having given Elizabeth a quick hug under Carleton's amused eyes before dinner, saying, "I could not be happier if I were marrying you myself!"

They went to Almack's, that pillar of propriety, on the Wednesday before the engagement party, as soon as a suitable outfit was ready for Elizabeth. It was a pale rose from Ellie's sample gowns, filled in around the neckline. The ladies made quite a stir at the venerable institution, arriving only minutes before the doors were closed, and with Carleton and Milbrooke in tow. The Duchess's infrequent visits alone were noteworthy, but these two handsome bachelors were virtual strangers at the gates. Miss Bethingame must be some prize, indeed, to have accomplished this! Everyone wanted to meet her, or at least get a close look at this new addition to the London scene, so she was the centre of a crowd throughout the evening after Carleton led her out in the opening quadrille and Ferddie had the second dance. She had no further opportunity to dance, through the constant introductions, which was how Sally Jersey had warned her it would be. Toward the end of the evening, however, Carleton spoke with his mother, then with Lady Jersey, who gave her nod to Elizabeth as a waltz was played. That Carleton should even have attended Almack's for Miss Bethingame's sake was enough for the gossips. When he requested—and received—permission for her to waltz at her debut there, the matter was clinched. The Duchess started to receive congratulations, which she did not bother to deny, with the formal betrothal only a day or so away.

Elizabeth knew she looked her finest for the ball—

everyone told her, Carleton's hand at her waist especially. He was in his satin knee-breeches and blue superfine, but had changed his diamond stickpin for a plain gold horseshoe which had belonged to Elizabeth's father, her engagement present to him. She was in a gown of palest yellow silk, with clusters of blue forget-me-nots embroidered on the bodice and scattered at the hem. She also had on the engagement ring, now sized to fit, and she showed it off proudly. The dinner guests toasted her health and happiness; Carleton lifted his glass, thanking them for all their kind wishes and proposed a toast himself, "to a certain horse, who had better win the Ardsley Cup, for all the haste and hurrying he is causing, but who has my eternal gratitude. Ladies and gentlemen, good luck to Folly's Pride." He kissed Elizabeth's cheek while the company laughed and clapped, before moving to the rooms cleared for dancing. This was not a huge crush like the country ball at Carlyle, and Elizabeth had already met most of the guests, so she was totally at ease, laughing and joking with Carleton's friends, accepting their extravagant compliments with good humour. In all she was happy, her dimples flickered delightfully—she was a great success.

"It's a good thing we're getting married so soon," Carleton teased when he took her hand for the first dance. "You might decide you would rather have one of your many admirers, if you had enough time to think about it."

"Oh, I've already had time for another offer, though I don't think it was for marriage, so you needn't worry about my reneging."

"Don't tell me you've received a proposition of that nature on the very day of our engagement! I can see I'll be calling out my own friends next. No, I will not ask who, I'll just smile and see who looks guilty."

Instead of staying with her in surveillance, though, he left her among a crowd of young men to pay his respects to other ladies. His parting words were, "Enjoy yourself, darling, save the waltz for me," which set the pattern for the next two weeks of her stay in London. At all the balls and dances she attended, no matter how many gentlemen were asking to dance, the waltz was always Carleton's. If she was already on the floor waiting for the music to start when a waltz began, she simply excused herself to her partner and waited for the Marquis to appear. Once she even refused Prinny himself, who laughed when she told him why. The Regent was so charmed by her he had the band play another waltz immediately, claiming his right to that one, at least. The tale was told all over London, increasing her consequence, until everyone was wanting to meet the Beauty who could chance offending Royalty without thinking twice.

Besides balls, the time was spent with more dress fittings and more conferences about the house, only now Elizabeth and Carleton went together to check the progress. He called for her in his high-perch phaeton and they drove in Hyde Park after the inspections, stopping constantly to greet acquaintances and accept congratulations. Carleton let Elizabeth take the reins a few times, only to be teased when his friends rode up to say that she was a finer whip than he.

"Just you wait," he told them, setting off again, "until you see her on horseback, then you'll know what a paragon she is!"

"But you have never seen me ride, Alexander, and I have no horse here in London."

"If you are not the finest horsewoman in London, the engagement is off." His eyes were twinkling as he went on: "Mother enquired. Your new riding habit should be ready tomorrow, so should your engagement present."

"A horse? Oh, Alexander, is it truly? I have been missing the horses so, and I was going to speak to you about sending for Ginger. I suppose I must ride sidesaddle, mustn't I?"

Carleton pulled the horses to a stop and slowly turned to her, his eyes searching her face for the joke. Big brown eyes only stared up at him innocently, so he said, "Miss Bethingame, you would not—you could not—be considering riding astride here, in front of the entire *ton*, would you? Dear God, say you never thought of it."

"Never, Lord Carleton, never." She batted her long brown eyelashes at him in the way of a silly flirt and they laughed together, then he kissed her, right there in front of the entire *ton*.

Elizabeth's new horse was wonderful, a large, spirited black mare to match Carleton's Jupiter, so they named her Juno, after the goddess of beginnings, birth and marriage. If Elizabeth wasn't the best horsewoman around, she decided after all the praise she won, at least she was the happiest.

She was not so well pleased with the day of her presentation at Buckingham Palace. It was a hot, dreary affair, made sufferable only by knowing she would never have to do it again. There was so little time before she returned home for the wedding she felt it was a shame to waste the day standing around or making curtsies when she could be getting to know Carleton better.

On their last evening in Town the Marquis took Elizabeth, Margaret and the Duchess to Vauxhall Gardens for the fireworks, hiring a boat to row them across the river for the best view. They met Milbrooke and Margaret's captain, and some of the Duchess's friends for a supper of oysters and lobster patties, then strolled around the gardens until it was time to leave.

"The next time you are here it will be as a married woman," Carleton told Elizabeth as he led her down a darkened pathway, the Duchess and her party some diplomatic yards behind.

"And will it be as beautiful the second time, or does one grow tired of it?" she asked.

"It will be more beautiful," he said, taking her in his arms and kissing her tenderly.

# TWELVE

The final week before the wedding was almost quiet for Elizabeth compared to her time in the city. Carleton was staying on to make sure the house was complete and would only arrive for the wedding dinner. There was tea with the Duchess and the local ladies, of course, and a pile of gifts to be acknowledged, but most of the details of the wedding itself were being handled by the staff at Carlyle. Elizabeth's new clothes had all been left in London for delivery to the Grosvenor Square house, except for her travelling clothes and her wedding gown, which would arrive with Ellie at the end of the week, so she had no need to see about much packing, only a few personal items she wished to take. A distant relative had come to stay while Elizabeth was in London, so even Aunt Claudia was content without her company. Cousin Faye was a ludicrous mismatch to Lady Burke, being tall, thin, afraid of dogs and disdainful of men. She did, however, love a good card game, and the two were involved in endless rounds of piquet, betting sums neither would ever see. Elizabeth's father's rooms had been redecorated for the Marquis, but the housekeeper had seen it all completed, with the additional staff newly hired, and Jackson had the repairs to the barns and stables well in hand, besides the Pride's training. Elizabeth really had very little to do, except worry.

She was not sure the Marquis would ever want to leave

London, where he was so gay and popular; he might decide he would rather stay at Carlyle Hall while they were in the country, with all its magnificent advantages, other than being his. They should have discussed these things more, but there had been so little time! They had not even been able to decide about a honeymoon trip because of the political uncertainty of the Continent. She knew she would be happiest to return here after the races outside London, if Carleton was with her, though she had no idea how he felt. That, of course, was her most distressing problem: Carleton had never said he loved her. He was happy in her company, she knew, but so was her dog! He was proud of her looks and pleased with her success, but this only gave her minor satisfaction, knowing the Marquis felt the same way about his new phaeton. No, he had never said in so many words that he was even glad to be marrying her. She would not be foolish enough to confess her love for him in this marriage of convenience while he, for all she knew, was still regretting the marriage altogether.

While not exactly regretting the entire marriage, Carleton was bidding a sad farewell to his bachelor days. He saw his belongings carried to Grosvenor Square and his household installed there, along with additions Henrys had hired with Elizabeth's approval. He'd moved to the Clarendon Hotel for two days where he, too, sat, worried over the future with a bottle of cognac for company. What if Elizabeth grew so fond of being the Storm of the Town that the country no longer interested her now that he had promised the Duke to take over some of the estate management? He knew she was caught up in her stables, but she had never known anything else. What if she lost her wonderful openness and became a typical shrew? Worst of all, in his mind, was the spectre of Elizabeth's many admirers. The thought of all those men hanging around her bothered him; more, the idea that she might fall in love and someday accept an offer from one of them. Carleton did not consider himself a jealous man, but he had never had anything like Elizabeth to cherish, to wish to guard so carefully. God, he thought, his life could be hell! He only wished he had had the courage enough to tell the girl he loved her, to see if she'd accept him on his own, without all the negotiations. He hated the damned contract now, although he had been so insistent about it. He poured himself another glass, then had a few with Ferddie when he called before the bachelor party.

The party was to begin at the hotel that night, and at Carleton's expense, since he was the first defector from the bachelor-brotherhood ranks. His friends assembled for toast after toast—two days' worth, from the hotel to the clubs to the taverns to the dives. They finally returned to the hotel at dawn, all who could stand.

"Northwell, what day is it?"

"It's your wedding day. We're celebrating it, ain't we?"

"No, it ain't been yet, Carleton, it's tomorrow."

"The wedding? Oh, Lord, I've got to get to Carlyle for the dinner. Ferddie, it's time, we've got to go."

Milbrooke staggered to his feet, asking someone to lift him into the saddle. Northwell propped him up by the door while Carleton poured out one more glass.

"A last toast, gentlemen." They all groaned. "To . . . to the name of my wife. I'll kill any sonofabitch who dishonours it."

Once again Carleton was riding pell-mell for Carlyle, this time with Ferddie weaving in the saddle beside him. They arrived with scant time to change for dinner and greet the guests: his Carleton relatives, Elizabeth's aunt and uncle, a few close neighbours and friends. He could only manage a weak smile for Elizabeth when she took one look at him at the door and said, "Heavens, Alexander, if you'd rather drink yourself to death than marry me, I'll call it off."

"Nonsense, nonsense," the Duke said, taking her arm. "They just got carried away. He'll be fine by the wedding."

But the dinner lasted eternally, it seemed, with more toasts, and Uncle Aubry wanted to stay up, chatting over his port after the other guests had departed and Ferddie and the Duke had retired, so Carleton was anything but fine on his wedding day. His head ached so much his hair hurt and his eyes refused to meet the glare of his mirror. Ainsley did what he could, though Elizabeth's Aunt Eunice still gave Carleton a disgusted look when they met on the way to the church.

Elizabeth was waiting when her uncle arrived to collect her, so he never had to step down from the open carriage. He silently handed her the bouquet of daisies she was to carry with her mother's bible. They were followed to the chapel by another carriage wth Aunt Claudia and Cousin Faye, and others for Ellie, Nanny, Bessie, Jackson and the servants. Everyone filed into the tiny chapel except Elizabeth and her uncle, who remained in the carriage while she placed flowers on the graves of her parents in the churchyard. Then Margaret came out to join her and at last the organ music started.

Elizabeth had only quick impressions of the chapel— the familiar faces smiling at her, the banks of flowers, Carleton standing stiffly at her side—before the ceremony was over and she was in the vestry, signing the licenses and contracts. Then she was caught up in warm embraces on her way to the carriage outside. The horses' manes and tails had been braided with ribbons, the carriage was filled with flowers, the local villagers she'd known all her life were tossing rose petals and shouting their good wishes. It was quite a procession to Carlyle Hall, all the carriages, all the people lining the roads; there was no chance for even a few quiet words between the bride and groom. When they reached Carlyle, all of that household was waiting outside with speeches by the butler and the head grounds-keeper, and then the tenants. The breakfast followed, with cake and champagne, and a small band playing, and everyone laughing and shouting at once. Finally Elizabeth went upstairs with Margaret, where the Duchess's woman helped her into her travelling outfit. Bessie had already been sent ahead with the baggage to the inn where the Carletons would spend their wedding night.

"Here, Margaret," Elizabeth said, handing over the lace veil. "You'll be next, so take good care of it."

"I only hope I make such a beautiful bride!" The two girls hugged each other affectionately before Elizabeth descended the staircase, to more cheers, more flowers and another carriage ride.

This time the carriage was the Duke's own closed chaise, four-horse team, crest and all. Elizabeth waved out of the window until they were out of sight, then she leaned back on the pillows.

"Well, at least we don't have to do that again," she said to her new husband as she turned to see why he was so quiet. He had finally found a comfortable place to rest his pounding head, against the soft pillows of the coach, and was fast asleep.

Carleton was still asleep when they stopped to change horses, so Elizabeth declined lunch, directing the coachman to drive straight through to the Unicorn Inn, where the Marquis finally stirred and apologised.

"You should have woken me. Lord, you must be famished. I am. Why don't you go wash while I see how soon dinner can be served."

Bessie was waiting upstairs in the suite the innkeeper's wife led Elizabeth to, so in no time at all she was ready to meet Carleton in the adjoining sitting room where a table had been set by the fireplace, amid candles and flowers. Champagne stood in buckets and Ainsley himself was waiting to serve them from covered dishes. They were both hungry; the food was excellent; Carleton's headache was at least bearable, yet thoughts of the night ahead made conversation between them awkward.

At last, the table cleared and the servants gone, Carleton leaned back in his chair.

"It's been a long day. Perhaps you would like to change out of your travelling clothes." His one-sided smile said a great deal more than his words.

Blushing, Elizabeth merely nodded before fleeing to her room. Carleton cursed himself for an ass, embarrassing her that way. Of course she was nervous; damn, wasn't he? He'd never dealt with an innocent before or, good Lord, a wife of his own! Here he was, still more than a little foxed and bone-weary, and about to make love to a chit of a girl who ran away from him blushing. What did he know of her, after all? Maybe she still didn't want to be married, especially to him. His hand trembled as he poured out another glass of champagne.

What Elizabeth really wanted was a bath, after the dust of the carriage ride and the hectic morning, so she sent Bessie off to fetch serving girls with a tub and cans of hot water. When they were gone, she undressed and lay back in the scented water.

"Here now, Miss Bitsy—your Ladyship, that is," Bessie teased. "You don't want to keep his Lordship waiting too long or he'll be a-knockin' the door down."

Elizabeth, wrapping warm towels around herself, laughed back and agreed to hurry. "But lock the door to the sitting room, Bessie, just in case. I don't want him to see me yet."

Bessie locked the door before coming to unpin Elizabeth's thick curls, brushing them out to fall softly around her shoulders. Then she held out the new negligée, gossamer-thin and lace-covered, admiring it again.

"Now wouldn't your uncle be pleased to know he paid for this?" Bessie giggled, and Elizabeth had to laugh out loud at the look she could just imagine on his face. Truly it was the most deliciously improper thing she had ever owned. She only hoped someone else would appreciate it.

Carleton, meanwhile, had gone to his own room to remove his stiff cravat, wash and put on his long brocade robe instead of a waistcoat. When he returned to the sitting room, he could still hear laughter and sounds of activity from Elizabeth's room so he pulled a chair closer to the fire and finished the bottle of champagne. He was gazing at the flames, thinking of how beautiful Elizabeth had looked in the chapel, how he was now a married man, how... What with the warmth of the room, the full dinner and not being entirely recovered from the past three days and nights, his head dropped forward on his chest. Only when the glass dropped out of his hand with a crash did he jerk up with a start. The fire was well down. God, what a fool I am, he told himself furiously, shaking his head to clear it from the wine and the nap. A little befuddled, he wondered if Elizabeth was angry at his neglecting her, or relieved. There was only one way to find out, he thought, and shoved his chair back and strode over to the connecting door.

Elizabeth was drowsing peacefully when she heard the glass break and the furniture move. The one candle she had left burning had gone out, so she could not tell how much time had passed. Startled awake, she groped for the matches when she heard Carleton's hand at the door—which was locked. She jumped out of bed but could not find her robe as the door rattled fiercely. She was about to call out when Carleton's angry words reached her through the door:

"What happened, madam, didn't *this* get written in your precious contract? Or was I too late and backward in my attentions to you? I should have known you would be like every other woman. You got what you wanted and the rest of the bargain be damned!"

It took Elizabeth a while to fumble with the key in the dark. By the time she was in the sitting room, Carleton's door was slamming and she could hear his footsteps stomping down the hallway. She tripped over his robe on the floor, pulling open the door he'd just slammed, but he was out of sight. She couldn't go charging after him through the corridors of a public inn, not dressed in a flimsy nightdress, so she softly, quietly shut the door and walked back to the sitting room. She pulled his robe around her and curled in a chair by the dying fire to wait for his return. It was cold though, and her legs were getting cramped. There were no more logs for the fire and still he did not come back. Eventually she gave up and found her own soft bed, thinking that they would have something to laugh about over breakfast.

Elizabeth slept late in the morning and she was annoyed. Bessie knew they had wanted to get an early start.

"No, Miss El—my Lady. His Lordship himself said there was no hurry," Bessie said while pulling the shades to let in the sunlight.

"Oh, well could you ask his Lordship to meet me in the sitting room in half an hour? There's been a misunderstanding, you see." She laughed nervously.

I'll say there's been a misunderstanding, Bessie said to herself, with the whole inn knowing his Lordship spent his wedding night in the public rooms, drinking himself lower than his boots. She started to fuss with Elizabeth's dress, not wanting to meet her eyes. "There's been a change of plans, ma'am. His Lordship's ridden ahead with the baggage. He says we're to follow whenever it's convenient."

It was a very small "oh" that echoed back from the bedclothes.

The staff of the Grosvenor Square house was all lined up to greet the new mistress in the hall. Mr. Sebastian, Carleton's secretary, made a polite speech expressing their hopes for her happiness in her new home. There were no toasts, cheers or flowers—no bridegroom either—only sympathetic looks for the pale young bride. Elizabeth changed, ate almost none of the cold luncheon provided for her, then lay down on her bed to rest and think. She had to see Carleton, but she could not search out the entire city for him, so there was nothing to do but wait, and listen to the servants tiptoeing past her room, most likely whispering about her. She went downstairs again and tapped on the door where Mr. Sebastian made his office.

"My Lady." He jumped up to hold the door for her. "What may I do for you?"

"I . . . I thought we might look over the wedding gifts. I . . . I can begin some of the acknowledgements."

The small sitting room had been cleared to display the glittering masses of presents, silver and crystal mostly, with a Sèvres vase in prominence on the mantle, a gift from Prinny himself. Elizabeth began to unwrap the newly delivered packages while a housemaid arranged the gifts sent up from the Folly. At first she enjoyed tearing away the silver paper—who doesn't like to get presents?—until the third comfit dish. She was content after that to let the maid open the boxes, exclaiming over each pair of candlesticks, while Elizabeth read the cards before handing them over to Mr. Sebastian for careful recording. Elizabeth might not ever have heard of Lord and Lady Rathbone, but she was duty-bound to thank them for the hideous teapot and not for the equally terrible fireplace dog. Turning to leave the room when the latest gifts were all open, Elizabeth caught sight of an enormous flat parcel in white paper.

"Whatever is that, Mr. Sebastian? At least it's not another tea service. It looks like a painting."

"No, my Lady. I believe it is—that is, I know it to be Lord Carleton's wedding gift to you. It was only delivered yesterday. I . . . I believe he had intended to give it to you himself."

"Yes, of course." She continued on her way out of the room.

There was no message from Carleton concerning dinner, so Elizabeth dressed in one of her new gowns, but he did not come. She had to eat in the long dining room all by herself. She did not have much appetite. Later she wandered around the quiet house, reading a few pages of a book here, playing a few chords on the piano there, ending in the small sitting room to look over the wedding gifts again. After a few minutes of contemplation, she turned and dragged Carleton's gift out to the centre of the room and propped it against the back of the sofa. She tore at a corner of the tissue, ripping it straight across to reveal, as she had thought, a large painting in a gilt frame—from the back. Annoyed and impatient, Elizabeth pulled the painting around to where she could see its front. She stood very still for a moment or two until, her eyes filled with tears, she could barely read the artist's signature. Whoever he was, in however short a time he must have had, he had done a magnificent portrait of Folly's Pride, with Elizabeth's home in the background. She slumped to the floor and, burying her face in her hands, she sobbed for hours.

# THIRTEEN

When Elizabeth came down to breakfast the next morning, the second since her marriage, the butler informed her that Lord Carleton would not return to dinner so she need not dress.

"What, was he here then, Henrys?"

"Yes, madam."

"And did you tell him I wanted to see him?"

"Yes, madam."

"And?"

"It was three o'clock in the morning, madam."

"What has that to do with anything? *My* butler would have called me!"

"Yes, madam." Henrys later told his wife they had better be looking for a new position. He could deal very well with the master, even in his cups as he was last night, and a black mood to boot, but a tiny young lady with dark shadows under her eyes, that was too much to ask of any respectable butler. Such a pretty little thing, too, he added.

Elizabeth spent the day inside again, keeping busy with the thank you's, picking at her food, watching the clock. She refused to eat dinner in the formal dining room again, ordering a tray sent to her room instead. After dinner she spent almost an hour in her study, composing a note to the Marquis. *Dear Lord Carleton,* it read, *I would hope we might resolve this foolish misunderstanding. Won't you please let me explain? If you are regretting our marriage so badly, I will return to the Folly as soon as I have made that explanation. Sincerely, Elizabeth.* She sealed the paper and handed it to Henrys with the admonition that *her* butler would not only see that Carleton got the note but would make sure that he read it.

"Yes, madam."

The note was still on the hall table when Elizabeth came down the third morning, after another sleepless night. Before she could discuss what her butler might have done, Henrys told her that the master had not come in at all. It almost burned his tongue to lie to the poor thing like that, but those were Carleton's orders. Henrys had tried to hand him the note on his way out again in fresh clothes, only the Marquis would have none of it. "No, I do not want any letters, and I cannot see her yet. If she thinks I am going to spend all of my days and nights in this house, going mad with wanting her, she can be damned. Tell her I was too drunk to read her letter; tell her I never came in; tell her to go home!" There was no way Henrys or his wife could think of to handle this without hurting the new mistress worse. He was not going to tell her the Marquis wished her to leave, so this seemed the best for now. Elizabeth went dejectedly back to her study to continue the correspondence. She would have to write to Aunt Claudia today, and the Duchess, though what she could say was beyond her.

About mid-morning Henrys knocked on the door. Elizabeth's eyes lit up when she saw the note on his tray until he announced that Lady Emilia Hazelton and Miss Darlinda Hazelton had come to leave their cards; was she receiving callers? Lady Hazelton was a bore, a gossipy chatterbox; Miss Hazelton was also a bore, though at least inoffensive, a quiet mouse. Elizabeth would never have seen them except that she'd seen no one in days, she hadn't been out of the house, she was edgy, restless, and already bored.

124

"Please ask them to come to the drawing room, Henrys."

"My dear Lady Carleton, I was so sorry to hear you are not feeling well," Lady Hazelton began as she took a seat. "And I see you are still not looking at all the thing. I wondered if we should call, since Carleton said you might be returning to the countryside to recuperate—so healthful—but then we received your kind note. I do hope you like green? I said to Darlinda, why, if Lady Carleton is well enough to write her thank-you's, surely she might like a visitor, didn't I, Darlinda?"

Miss Hazelton nodded.

"I told Carleton, too, last night at the theatre. I said I'm sure you'd like a little company, but you know how men are. Lord Hazelton was always the same, one sniffle and he'd be out of the house. Couldn't bear suffering, he said. Lady Gilmore also sends her regards."

"How kind, Lady Hazelton, thank you very much for coming. You were right, a little company has done wonders for my health."

So Carleton was telling everyone she was sick, was he, while he was at the theatre with Alicia Gilmore, whose husband was with the Foreign Office somewhere. Elizabeth stalked out to the hall, took her note to Carleton off the table and slowly, precisely, tore it to shreds. She neatly placed the bits in Henrys's tray, then asked him to have her horse brought round in half an hour.

Juno was skittering around outside when Elizabeth returned in a gold velvet riding habit. Jeremy, Carleton's groom, was at the horse's head; another horse, also saddled and ready, stood quietly by.

"I did not ask for a groom to accompany me, Henrys."

"No, madam."

"If I requested you to have him stay home, would you listen to me?"

"No, madam."

She smiled, the first time Henrys had seen her dimples. "You know, Henrys, that is precisely what *my* butler would have said."

Jeremy, who'd never actually seen her Ladyship ride though he'd been driving her in the carriage, warned her of the black's high spirits. "She's a mite skittish, ma'am. Needs a good run, I'd say."

"Then that's what she shall have." Elizabeth was holding Juno to a sedate trot, allowing Jeremy to mount and catch up, until she reached the park. So close to luncheon was not a fashionable time for the *ton* to be riding, so for once the paths were not blocked. All Elizabeth had to do was lean forward a bit and whisper in Juno's ear; they were off and almost out of Jeremy's sight, a gold and black blur.

"C'mon, you old nag you," Jeremy called to his horse as he urged him on with his heels. "We'll never catch 'em, but at least let's 'ave the pleasure a watchin' 'er Ladyship ride!"

A few other visitors to the park also had the pleasure. Two old dowagers watched her gallop around their ancient brougham. "Isn't that the girl young Carlyle married?" one asked. After Jeremy struggled past, the other answered: "And in remarkable good health, wouldn't you say?"

By chance Lord Milbrooke had also been on a solitary ride in the park, trying to clear a head misted with too much drink and not enough sleep. He was letting his mount pick its own way home when Elizabeth flew by on Juno, her hair trailing undone behind her, her skirts in disarray. Ferddie pulled his horse around, thinking to go to her rescue, when she reined the black mare in and turned her back, in perfect control.

"Why, good morning, Lord Milbrooke. I didn't expect to see you," she said, drawing up to him.

"No, I daresay you didn't. Where is your groom?"

She laughed as she bent to smooth her skirts. "He's right behind me, all perfectly proper."

"Good grief, Elizabeth, what have you done to yourself?" he asked when she straightened and he could see her face. She looked like a waif, with the dark smudges under her big brown eyes, the bones of her cheeks standing out in her pale face. She turned away, as if searching in her pockets for a hairpin. Ferddie was instantly sorry for his words; he only wished he could think of something else to say. "I suppose you'll be going to the Haversham ball tonight now that you're out and about? Everyone is, I guess."

"No, I don't—that is, Carleton hasn't—Ferddie, are you going? Would you take me, please?"

Now I've done it, Ferddie thought. He could either say he wasn't going—and be caught in a lie if she came—or say he did not want to take her. He knew things were bad between her and Carleton; he didn't know why and he didn't want to be in the middle. Yet here was Elizabeth looking up at him like an abandoned puppy. He was genuinely fond of her, and she really had no friends in Town, and Carleton could be damned cruel when his temper was riled.... "My pleasure, I'm sure." He was rewarded with a wide smile as Jeremy finally appeared, then they parted, with Milbrooke wondering where Carleton had holed up, so he could warn him.

Milbrooke was never able to run Carleton to ground though he left notes at the clubs, which dimmed his pleasure in seeing Elizabeth in better looks that evening. She had slept a little—more from exhaustion than any purposeful coddling of her appearance—and Bessie had applied some cosmetic assistance to her unnatural pallor. She was nervous. Almack's had not fazed her, nor Buckingham Palace; this made her tremble. Ferddie, who also had reason to be uneasy over the evening, nevertheless took her hand as they reached the receiving line.

"Ah, Lady Haversham, see whom I've brought! You do know Lady Carleton, don't you?"

"Indeed, Lord Milbrooke," she said, kissing Elizabeth's cheek, "and I am delighted you have come. When Carleton said you were still not up to socialising I was quite concerned, but you have relieved me greatly."

Elizabeth murmured something about feeling quite well, thank you, so kind, before Ferddie was able to lead her away. He took a handkerchief and wiped his forehead. He knew Carleton would come; Alicia Gilmore wouldn't miss a chance like this to show off her new prize. Perhaps Elizabeth might never see them. Lord, in such a crush anything was possible. On the other hand, he considered, maybe she and Carleton could resolve their difficulties if they met out in company, having a civilised talk in one of the side-rooms like the reasonable people he knew they weren't. At any rate, he could not see the Marquis yet, although a group of their friends was beckoning. He led Elizabeth to them, where she was warmly received, touched by their concern for her health, supposedly. Ferddie asked Northwell about his new team of bays when he sensed Elizabeth's growing embarrassment. Lord, he thought, this chaperoning was a touchy business. The pair of horses had to be described for Elizabeth, who turned out to know an anecdote about the stables they had come from, so soon everyone was laughing and joking, to Ferddie's relief. He led her out for the first dance, with still no sign of Carleton. Rutley had the second dance, Northwell the third. Ferddie was keeping a watchful eye as other, younger men approached her until he saw she could handle herself. In fact, he could almost hear the hearts dropping at her feet. Her laugh was a little forced, and her eyes had no golden sparkle, but the girl was learning to flirt. Nevertheless, by unspoken consent, Carleton's friends stayed close to her, unobtrusively shielding her from any unwelcome advances. If anyone had asked them, they would have claimed loyalty to Carleton as the reason, though if truth be known, they were jealously protecting their own enjoyment. Elizabeth was still a novelty to Northwell, Rutley and the others in that she was intelligent and witty, involved in their own interests, and safe. Her company among them was a good reflection, without being a threat to their bachelorhoods or purses. These friends of Carleton's were no longer green youths, hanging out for a wife; nor were they remotely considering her as a mistress. The companionship of a beautiful, intelligent woman who would not question their intentions, that was a rarity indeed. The time passing pleasantly, Milbrooke felt free to leave Elizabeth for his duty-dances, though it might take him a while to cross the crowded room. As he strolled toward where he'd last seen his hostess, he saw Carleton re-entering the ballroom through the glass doors of the balcony, with Lady Alicia Gilmore on his arm. Milbrooke turned in that direction, but Lady Haversham grabbed his sleeve and was about to present him to a drab girl at her side when the music began, a waltz.

A number of people must have seen Carleton enter for Elizabeth's admirers, especially Carleton's friends, so used not to asking her to waltz, all stood aside. A few even wandered off to seek other partners, leaving Elizabeth with an unobstructed view of her husband raising Lady Gilmore's hand to his lips and kissing it before leading her onto the floor. Whatever polite apologies or explanations Elizabeth had wanted to make melted like snow in the heat of the words on her tongue. The insult, the shame of standing there.... She made to leave but her path was blocked by a stranger in a black waistcoat with lace at his throat.

"*Madame*, may I have the pleasure of the dance?" he asked. Elizabeth was too distracted to notice anything more than the French accent.

"No, thank you, I must leave."

"What, like a whipped dog?"

Elizabeth lifted her eyes from the floor, at first outraged by this stranger's presumption, then acknowledging the wisdom behind his taunt. "No, *monsieur*, not like a whipped dog. I am pleased to have this dance. *Merci.*"

He bowed low, introducing himself as Giles Jean-Christophe, le Comte de Rochefonte.

"How is it we have not met, *monsieur?*" Elizabeth asked, determined to pretend Carleton's nonexistence, though the look of his face smiling at Alicia Gilmore was burnt in her memory.

"Ah, *madame,* "the Count answered as he led her out, "I am not often introduced to young ladies, although I know their fathers and brothers well."

"I don't understand, *monsieur.*" Elizabeth looked closely at her partner for the first time after this curious statement. She saw dark, dark eyes in a sombre face that was more interesting than handsome, with its deep lines and harsh planes. She guessed de Rochefonte was about forty, older than most of the men she knew, with more experience of life, too. Suffering showed in the shadows of his eyes, and something else behind it.

"I am afraid I am considered too dangerous company for young maidens. I am thought to be a fortune-hunter." He spoke seriously, not in the bantering, flirtatious tone she was used to hearing tonight, and his words startled her, that he might know of her own still-maidenly state. She stiffened a little in arms, which told him what he had suspected, before she asked, "And *are* you a fortune-hunter, sir?"

"Alas, Lady Carleton, I am forced to be," he admitted ruefully. "I have lost everything to Napoleon but my name. If I wish even that to outlast him in hopes of returning to claim what is ours, I must marry; yet I cannot afford a mere wife, only an heiress. You see"—he smiled slightly, a quick shadow-lifting—"I am honest, at least."

Elizabeth was not offended. In fact, since she was not an heiress, and married besides, she could be sympathetic. Who was she to disdain a marriage of convenience? If he arrived penniless at some rich man's door, at least he possessed an elegance and a nobility missing in the typical English lordling.

When the dance was over de Rochefonte returned her to her friends. "*Au revoir, madame*, perhaps another time—" but Rutley cut in with his request for the next dance. When Elizabeth turned around, the Count was separated from her by smiling young faces.

Milbrooke, meanwhile, was detained from hurrying to her side by yet another hand on his sleeve—this one in blue superfine, with a sapphire signet ring. Carleton was furious, Ferddie saw, as he followed him out to the balcony.

"Well?" Carleton demanded.

"I tried to warn you—left notes all over. She asked me to take her. How could I refuse?"

"I am not referring to my wife's presence here. I am referring to de Rochefonte and well you know it."

And he did, too, know what an unsuitable companion the Count was for Elizabeth, yet the injustice of Carleton's words stung him. "Well, I didn't see you doing anything about it! For all anybody'd know, you couldn't care at all whom she danced with."

"But I didn't bring her, you did."

"Dammit, she's your wife!"

"Precisely why I do not care to have *monsieur le Comte* near her."

Something clicked in Ferddie's mind. "God, he's not Yvette's Frenchman, is he?"

Carleton nodded, his lips in a grim line. "He can look for another pigeon to pluck if he wants, but not as high as my wife."

"Yes, well, you know she's only a girl; she ain't been in Town long. Maybe you ought to look after her yourself...."

"She'll do fine until the races, then home she goes."

"Aren't you being hard on her, Carleton? I don't know—"

"No, you don't, so leave it be."

Ferddie was familiar with these tempers of Carleton's from their school days. He would forget about his anger tomorrow; tonight there was no reasoning with him. Milbrooke moved toward the door back to the ballroom. "I'll see what I can do about the Count. I'll—"

"We've already seen what you can do. I'll speak to Elizabeth myself." Carleton walked off, not toward his wife and his friends but out to where punch was being served. Ferddie spotted Elizabeth dancing with Reggie Skeffington so he had time before she came back for a few words with Rutley and Northwell, who in turn looked over their shoulders and nodded. The ranks closed up a bit around Elizabeth at the next interlude. A young cousin of Northwell's who was looking at Elizabeth adoringly was sent to fetch some punch. She agreed with Ferddie that perhaps she should sit out the next dance or two since she was supposed to have been quite ill. As a matter of fact, Elizabeth was exhausted and depressed. She was just about to ask Ferddie to take her home after the next dance when the orchestra again began a waltz. This time everyone was ready, five men immediately asking for the dance. Milbrooke claimed priority, making light of it by joking about his role as dance instructor. "I taught her to dance, you know. Tell them it's true, Elizabeth."

"Only the waltz! And you kept comparing me to a chair, Ferddie!" They were all laughing again on easy terms when a deep voice broke in: "I believe this dance is mine."

Elizabeth nodded, "My Lord," excused herself to Ferddie and preceded Carleton to the floor. Ferddie went off to find a partner, relaxed now that his burden of responsibility would be lifted.

Elizabeth did not know where to begin. She was hurt, angry, jealous—and thrilled to be in Carleton's arms again. "Alex—"

"My Lady, if you wish to go out, I shall be happy to oblige you," he said stiffly. "There is no need to bother Ferddie."

132

Anger won the toss. "How dare you! When I have been trying to reach you for days and you won't see me? Ferddie said he was pleased to take me, so you—"

"Furthermore, my Lady, I do not approve of your choice of partners in Giles de Rochefont."

"Well at least he does not dampen his dress to cling in a revolting manner like your choice of partner."

"Hardly. But my partner has never abducted a young girl in hopes of forcing her parents' consent to their wedding."

If this was true, and she could not believe Carleton would lie to her, it was indeed reprehensible, yet she could not, of course, admit this to Carleton. His insufferable arrogance was making her do and say things she had never wanted. "Since I am already married, sham though it is, I do not see where your vile accusations concern me."

A muscle in Carleton's jaw was twitching, as from teeth held clenched too long. "As you say, madam, sham though it is, we are married, and I say I do not like him."

"Then do not dance with him." She stopped dancing. "I shall see whom I want. In the Count, at least, I shall know why he is interested."

"What is that supposed to mean?" he snapped.

"It means, my Lord, that if you only married me to share my bed, then good riddance!" There, she had said it, the horrible fear she'd had, the only explanation she could think of for his irrational behaviour over the door. She hated herself for saying it, repulsed by the whole idea. Unable to face him again, she stomped off, leaving Carleton standing in the middle of the dance floor, looking like a fool to all those fortunate enough to witness this latest incident in the already colourful courtship. The Carleton Affair, as it was generally referred to, was considered by the gossips to be the major item of the Season. Another chapter was about to be written. It might have gone differently, except for the crowds, because Carleton, momentarily stung by her words, had recovered and was pushing through the other couples to go after her. Elizabeth, meanwhile, could find neither Milbrooke nor her other friends where she had left them, only one familiar, dark-shadowed face:

"*Tout à vous, madame.* At your service."

Elizabeth rode out early the next morning, again leaving Jeremy behind at the park's gates. There was a thick mist, however, forcing her to hold Juno in check lest she chance an accident. No one was in sight, with only the steady dripping from the leaves to disturb her thoughts. She was considering returning to the country. After last night, everyone in London would know that her marriage was a failure; there was no use remaining to pretend otherwise. Yet the races would be held just outside London, in a few short weeks, and the Pride would be brought up soon, in slow stages, so he could be rested. She had to be here fore that. . . .

"*Bon jour, madame.*" A dark figure on a mist-coloured horse materialised from the woods to her left. Elizabeth slowed Juno, looking over her shoulder, wishing Jeremy would hurry. This was wildly improper, she knew, even though unintentional, somehow worse than leaving the ball with him last night. He had behaved with perfect propriety, hardly a word being spoken on the ride to Grosvenor Square. The Count had not even got down from the carriage at her door. Still, she could not be easy with him after reflecting on Carleton's tale. She could not simply ride past him, either, especially after his kindness to her, so she pulled up to wait for her groom, noting that the Count looked more melancholy by daylight, less mysterious.

"Good morning, *monsieur*, you are out early. I do not recall if I thanked you properly for your assistance last evening. I . . . I was not thinking clearly."

"Or else you would never have gone with me, eh, *madame?*"

His intuitiveness continued to surprise her. She decided to risk matching his bluntness with her own, if only for her peace of mind. "Is it true, *monsieur*, this story I hear of an abduction?"

"Alas, an ill-conceived act of desperation. Please believe me, *madame*, the lady was never harmed. In fact, she is now happily wed to her childhood sweetheart, so some good came of it. You do not fear me, do you? You are already married, *oui*? And you are not an heiress, regrettably. And, finally, your husband is too fine a marksman for me to tempt Fate, *madame*. Ah, here is your groom. I bid you good day, my Lady Carleton."

The hall was filled with flowers when Elizabeth arrived home.

"My Lady must have had an enjoyable evening last night, if I might say so," Henrys commented as he handed her a parcel of letters and cards.

"No, I am just a curiosity," she replied, glancing at the tags on the flowers. There were bouquets from most of her partners, a few from complete strangers. "Did...did my Lord—"

"Oh, yes, madam. Lord Carleton wished me to inform you that he will not be dining at home; he has a box for the theatre and asks that you be ready for nine o'clock, if that is agreeable. He also mentioned that you might speak with Mr. Sebastian about any invitations you would care to accept. And Lord Milbrooke is in the sitting room. He said he would wait."

Ferddie greeted her with the warmth of an old friend, she was relieved to see, complimenting her on the décor of the rooms.

"Thank you, Ferddie, I have been thinking of having some form of entertainment, to show the house off. Ferddie, you are not angry with me about last night, are you?"

"It is one of the things I wanted to see you about. Damn, Elizabeth, you can't go around acting screw-loose like that. It just ain't done."

"I know, Ferddie, I really do. It was deplorable to leave Carleton standing there like—"

"Carleton? No, he probably deserved being made the fool. I wanted to call him out myself last night. No, what I'm saying's not right was your leaving with the Count fellow. I brought you and I should have been the one to take you home. Besides, he ain't quite the thing."

"Oh, Ferddie, you are such a dear. The Count assured me that I am safe in his company since I am married. He is quite kind, you know." She did not mention her encounter of this morning, having no desire to hear another lecture, even from Ferddie. He cleared his throat, unwilling to go into details of the Frenchman's character.

"The other reason for my call—I would have come in any case, of course—was to ask if I could take you up in my phaeton this afternoon. Devering's challenged Northwell's new chargers and I thought you might like to watch."

"Thank you, Ferddie, I would, truly. But I don't want to—that is, Carleton said I mustn't bother you."

"Bother? Carleton's got some deuced queer notions these days. I want your advice on my pair's chances against Northwell's. Will you come?"

"What a good friend you are, Ferddie. Of course I'll come."

Northwell's pair won, of course. They really were a fine team. Elizabeth and Ferddie reluctantly agreed that his chestnuts were outmatched. They would make a run for it, but she advised Milbrooke not to put any money on the outcome. Carleton's bays could do it, however....

There was another couple in the carriage with the Marquis at nine o'clock, Baron and Lady Westron, so conversation was general and polite. Elizabeth was quick to take advantage of this:

136

"By the by, Alexander, would you mind if Jeremy took me out with the bays and the phaeton someday? I've noticed more ladies drive than ride. Don't you agree, Lady Westron?"

Carleton looked at her quizzically but acquiesced, going so far as to say he would ask Mr. Sebastian to keep an eye out for a suitable pair for her own. Nothing more was said on the matter, in fact nothing more was said to one another by the Carletons for the duration of the play. At the interludes Elizabeth's admirers filled the box; Carleton took himself off. After the theatre the group moved to a party at Regency Square. Elizabeth was again surrounded, but her husband was obviously not among her admirers. She laughed and danced and flirted, working hard to prove what a good time she was having. She had the first waltz with Ferddie, so there was no embarrassment. Carleton appeared for the second, later in the evening.

"This is merely for appearance sake, madam, so you can save the chit-chat for your retinue," he informed her at the start, never looking at her. She would have broken away, but his hand on her waist tightened. "No, not again," he said through clenched teeth. The dance was performed in stony silence, except for Carleton's parting words that he would see her home, at her convenience—another reproof of her last night's behaviour.

As soon as he had left her with his friends—her friends now—she issued a challenge to Northwell, his team against Carleton's bays.

"I thought he wasn't interested," Northwell began.

"No, but I am. Or are you ashamed to accept a challenge from a woman?"

"Does Carleton know?"

"I have his permission," she said, bending the truth of course, for he had said Jeremy might take her out, knowing nothing about a race. The event was scheduled for the following day to leave less time, she felt, for Carleton to stop it if he found out. She glanced his way somewhat guiltily to see him laughing happily with Lady Gilmore, which instantly decided Elizabeth she needed a good night's rest. An embarrassed Rutley was sent to inform the Marquis of his wife's wishes. The carriage might have been a hearse for all the conversation, nor did Carleton move when Henrys helped his wife alight. The coach went off.

Jeremy was called to Elizabeth's study early the next morning, but he was having none of it.

" 'Is Lordship left word how I was to take you out, ma'am, not about any race and not about any woman drivin', beggin' your pardon, ma'am."

"But he didn't say I couldn't either, did he?" Elizabeth knew it was Jeremy's vanity talking; how would he look to his mates with her at the reins? She appealed to his pride, though, since the bays' reputation was at stake. At last he agreed, reluctantly, and only because he knew the Marquis was already out.

"This one time only, ma'am, and we better win."

Mr. Sebastian was sent for next to advance Elizabeth a fairly large sum from her allowance—the stakes money, although he was not to know it. He took the opportunity of informing Elizabeth of Carleton's plans for the evening, a dinner party for eight o'clock. It would take some doing, with the race set for dusk when the park would be least crowded, but Elizabeth would wear her gown to the meet, if need be. Bessie could not be told where her mistress was off to after tea; she would have been horrified—nice young ladies surely did not race chariots in the park—although she would not have been surprised. Instead, she was merely informed that Lord Milbrooke was taking her to look at some horses again so there would be a rush before dinner, unless everything was laid out. Bessie clucked her tongue. There was an awful lot wrong going on here, with Elizabeth more lively than she'd been in days.

Bessie was relieved to have Elizabeth home in even better spirits, actually laughing during the frenzied dressing. She had not won the race—it was a tie—but she had done well, well enough to be happily proud, especially with all the approval she'd won. Milbrooke thought the Marquis himself could not have done better; Northwell admitted he'd had to do his damnedest just to tie her; Jeremy, even Jeremy, said they would have won with a few more feet to go. He gave her a wink, saying he'd be able to meet the fellows for a wet, after all. Elizabeth privately believed she could have won easily if she'd had a bit more practice with the bays. Nevertheless, the tie had given a boost to her image of herself, which had been suffering badly recently under Carleton's disdain. Her confidence only began to waver as Bessie tucked a last flower in her hair at exactly eight o'clock and Elizabeth had to face him.

A quick glance at his stormy expression told her he knew about the race and was furious: the eyebrows drawn low over his eyes, the jutting chin... "Would you mind terribly if I stayed home, my Lord? My... my head aches." He merely snatched her wrap from Henrys, threw it over her shoulders and led her to the waiting coach. She sat against one side, steeling herself for the harsh words. None came, however, though Carleton's mouth stayed fixed in a sneer. If he was not going to bring the subject up, Elizabeth was certainly willing to accept another silent carriage ride. Milbrooke and the other witnesses to the race could also read Carleton's expression, so the event was not mentioned until, separated from the Marquis by the length of the dinner table, Elizabeth was again regaled with praise in a continuing spirit of cheerful fellowship. When the gentlemen rejoined the ladies in the drawing room, however, after their port and cigars, it was a fairly subdued group which gathered at Elizabeth's side, obviously chastened. The pleasure was taken from the evening for Elizabeth who, despite the consequences, was prepared to have it out with Lord Carleton on the ride home.

"You had no right to say anything to Ferddie and the others, my Lord. If you were angry, the fault was mine and no one else's. It is unjust of you to —"

"No, my Lady, I laid the blame precisely where it was due. If you do not know any better, my *friends* do." He grimaced at the word. "And as for you, madam," he said as the coach stopped at their door and she stepped down, "my horses would have won if you had not held them so tight at the turn."

After that Elizabeth's days fell into a routine of sorts. She took Juno to the park in the early morning, careful to stay in Jeremy's sight, sometimes meeting the Count, more often not, returning home for morning callers and correspondence. She drove with one of her friends in the afternoon, paid calls or went shopping. If Carleton had not left plans for the evening with Mr. Sebastian, Ferddie or one of the others would ask to escort her somewhere. There was a constant round of dinners, balls, masquerades. Elizabeth attended them all, finding her own company oppressive. She began to give small teas, at first just to fill the hours, then for the pleasure of having people she knew around her. Occasionally she invited de Rochefonte, never when the other guests included unmarried women. Soon her gatherings had the reputation of being intelligent and amusing, with few people declining an invitation. Carleton never attended, despite the dates being carefully logged with Mr. Sebastian. Elizabeth never saw her husband except at evening functions where they arrived together, had one waltz, and left together, with not an extra word or smile. They never took meals together at home, nor had any private conversations, all of their dealings being done through the servants. Elizabeth had no idea where her husband went all day and most of the nights, although rumours reached her aplenty, coupling his name with that of Alicia Gilmore, the occasional singer, dancer and what you will. He was as driven as she was to find company, any company, and got as little rest. They were both exhausted, mentally as well as physically, from the emotional drain of this silent warfare. They kept going, telling themselves it was only till the races, only until Elizabeth could return home. Time was running short.

# FOURTEEN

The day Elizabeth received word that the Pride had finally arrived at the racetrack, along with Robbie Jackson, two grooms and the jockey, she begged Ferddie to drive her out. They made a party of it, Rutley inviting Miss van Houten to ride in his carriage. Elizabeth had a long conference with Robbie while the others walked around the stables, surveying the competition. The Pride was in fine shape, not disturbed by the trip in the least. Robbie had brought his own feed from home in another wagon and had even taken along one of the Folly's ponies, to give him some familiar company. One of the grooms slept outside the stall; no chances were being taken. This would be the only visit Elizabeth could manage before the race—the Duke and Duchess were arriving in two days, and Elizabeth was holding a party the race night—and she did not want it to end. Finally Ferddie had to pull her away so they could get home for dinner. As it was, Carleton had to hold the carriage for fifteen minutes before she was ready. She did not even notice his glare. Everyone except Carleton, of course, wanted to hear about the horses. Elizabeth stayed at the party longer than she had planned. The next day she could barely make herself get out of bed, Bessie fussing the entire time until she agreed to forego Juno's morning exercise. Instead Elizabeth haunted the kitchens, interfering with Mrs. Henrys's preparations for the party,

Elizabeth's first formal entertainment. It would be either a victory celebration or a consolation party, with all of her friends, but especially the Duke and Duchess and the group they were bringing to London. This included Margaret and Captain Hendricks, and Margaret's parents and brother Robert, with Miss Sophie Devenance and her mama. Everything had to be perfect, at least. Extra staff had been hired, outfitted and trained; special wines ordered; the menu changed daily. There was even a surprise entertainment planned for after dinner to add more excitement to the evening. Elizabeth had spent days with Mr. Sebastian over the guest lists, trying to combine her friends with her social obligations. Carleton had given Mr. Sebastian a list of ten names or so, most of which Elizabeth had already included. Lady Alicia Gilmore's name had been summarily crossed through on the grounds that since Carleton's family was so well represented, Elizabeth's friends took precedence. After the slightest hesitation, Giles de Rochefonte's name had been added to the final list. All of the acceptances were in, so that afternoon Elizabeth and Mr. Sebastian worked out seating charts. The Count offered a special problem, of course, that and the fact that most of Elizabeth's friends were men. What caused the most difficulty was the need of an alternate, contingency plan, if Carleton did not come. Elizabeth refused to face an empty seat if the Marquis decided to avenge Lady Gilmore's slight. By evening the cards had been juggled every which way, Mr. Sebastian as frazzled as Elizabeth, but two separate arrangements agreed upon. She was having dinner alone in the breakfast parlour, where she had taken to eating when at home rather than her bedroom or the huge dining table, when Henrys cleared his throat at the door.

"Excuse me, madam, but there is a Mr. Jackson to see you. He says it is urgent." Elizabeth dashed out of the room while Henrys looked on disapprovingly. She returned some time later as twitchy as a rabbit's whisker, he told his wife, explaining why the entire dinner was returned cold and uneaten.

Even Carleton noted her distress when he picked her up in the carriage for the opera. He had scrupulously avoided giving any notice to her appearance for the past weeks. Now he was dismayed by how gaunt and wan she looked.

"We need not go tonight if you would rather stay home, you know." Those were his kindest words to her in the same weeks. She hardly heard them.

"What's that? No, I must see Ferddie." She turned to look out the window again, missing the despair which showed in Carleton's eyes for a moment, to be replaced by his now-customary bitter, sarcastic expression. His frown deepened when, arriving at the party, Elizabeth rushed off to take Ferddie's hands, leading him to a secluded corner. No one interrupted them, not even when the first dance began. Carleton walked toward Rutley and Northwell only to have their conversation cut off at his approach; Devering looked at the Marquis coldly before turning his back to him. Carleton walked to the terrace and around the garden for a while. When he returned, Elizabeth was dancing with some young cub in high shirt collars and Milbrooke was alone by the punch bowl.

"Ferddie, I've got to leave. Would you see Elizabeth home?"

"Of course."

"She wouldn't listen to me, you know, but perhaps you could convince her to leave early. She's not looking very well...."

"Oh, so you noticed that, did you?" Ferddie asked reproachfully, moving off to intercept Elizabeth and her partner at the end of the dance. Carleton left, and shortly after Milbrooke and Elizabeth. Ferddie did not notice Carleton standing in the shadows of some trees across from the house, and Elizabeth hardly knew she was home until

Henrys took her wrap. Ferddie stood by when she asked if there was any word from Jackson, then made her promise to go straight to bed and stop worrying. He had a few words with Henrys, who was also gravely concerned, then left. When he saw Milbrooke leave after only five minutes, a great weight lifted from Carleton's mind, out there in the shadows. At least one person would rest easier that night.

The Duke and Duchess of Carlyle were coming to London for the Ardsley Cup races, which meant so much to their daughter-in-law, they said. They were actually coming because of all the rumours filtering back from Town. They had all of Elizabeth's letters, of course, and news from her Aunt Claudia about all the routs, fêtes and festivities of the Season; they also had news of Alicia Gilmore, unsavoury French counts, awkward scenes in public. The Duke was prepared to discount the stories as mere gossip at first, the idle lies of idle people; then his own cook's son returned from an errand in London where he had visited his mother's relatives, the Henrys. According to the Duke's informant, the butler, Alexander never ate home and hardly slept there. In ten minutes letters were sent to open the Berkeley Square house; the Duke was packing.

When the Carlyles arrived in London en masse, they had a quick luncheon then separated, the Duke going to his clubs, Margaret, Sophie and their mothers visiting the shops, and the Duchess paying a call on Elizabeth. They would dine in Berkeley Square, then go on to the theatre.

The Duchess was greeted warmly by Henrys, yet when she asked how things were at the house he mentioned a drafty chimney and a neighbour with barking dogs. Disgusted, she sent him to tell Elizabeth she had arrived. She was waiting in the small sitting room, admiring the way the room now looked, when Henrys opened the door for Elizabeth. The minute the Duchess saw her daughter-in-law she knew all of the rumours were true, and worse. She hugged the girl to her, mentally wringing her son's neck at the same time.

"Elizabeth, dear, it is so good to see you. Are you sure you are feeling well though?"

"Of course, your Grace. I have been so busy getting ready for tomorrow night, and then there has been some trouble with the horse. You know how much this means to me...."

"Has Alexander been any help?"

"Help? Why, yes, he's... he's stayed out of my way." It was the first thing to come to Elizabeth's mind; the Duchess smiled weakly.

"I still don't think you look very healthy, my dear. In fact, I think you would do better to stay in tonight, with tomorrow such an important day. I'm sure the Duke will be disappointed, but he would rather see you at your prettiest at the races. No, don't argue; I insist. You are not to come this evening, I'll tell Alexander myself." She did not say precisely what she would tell Alexander, but she was determined to see the girl get some rest, then have a few blunt words with her son. She made sure Elizabeth went upstairs, then left a note for Carleton with the butler.

That note put the finishing touch on another awful day for the Marquis. He had been cut dead by another of his friends, had an unpleasant row with Alicia Gilmore over not getting her invited to the coming party, and was in general suffering from feelings of guilt and remorse. He certainly did not need his mother to tell him that he was to blame, for whatever cause, for Elizabeth's misery. He had taken a happy, spirited country girl and brought her to London to be—what? Sickly, down-hearted, lonely—no, not lonely, judging from all the bouquets in the hall. There was every size of horseshoe made of flowers, "Good Luck" spelled out in carnations, messages of all kinds tied to the arrangements. It looked like Elizabeth would ruin the odds on her horse, with so many well-wishers. He smiled ruefully as he considered a totally unknown horse going off at even odds simply because its mistress was such a favourite of Society. The smile left as he read the card on a small bouquet of miniature roses: *Bon chance, de R.* His mother's note brought him still less joy. It advised him not to disturb Elizabeth under any conditions but to arrive somewhat early to dinner, as the Duchess wished a few words with him. He was not looking forward to this evening at all, nor to the day of the race and the party, when he and Elizabeth would have to put on a charade. He arrived at Carlyle House late, not early, and greeted his family cordially. He remarked somewhat pointedly on his father's well-being, following such a strenuous trip.

"You don't sound pleased to find me in good health, Alexander," the Duke replied.

"Your health pleases me greatly, sir. It is your scruples which worry me," he said, leading his mother's good friend Lady Palmerson in to dinner. He sat between Lady Palmerson and his cousin Margaret at table, avoiding his mother's eye. The gentlemen stayed long over their port, discussing the race, naturally, and immediately on joining the ladies Carleton excused himself to return to Elizabeth. If he could not put the Duchess off for long, at least this evening was past.

Henrys informed him that her Ladyship was resting, according to her woman, although another groom had been over with a package from Jackson. No, he did not know the contents. Carleton had to be content with that, figuring to question Elizabeth on the way to the track. They would leave about ten, picking up Ferddie and some of the others before joining the carriages with the Duke's party.

The following morning, however, Bessie was waiting outside his door. Her mistress was not up to attending the races; he would have to make her excuses. Oh, no, Bessie said, he must not go in to her as she had finally fallen asleep after a restless night. Carleton could not believe Elizabeth would miss this day unless she was on death's door. He was ready to send for a doctor. No, Bessie assured him, she did not think it terribly serious, only that her Ladyship wanted to be feeling better for the dinner party. He was not at all satisfied; something else besides worry was nibbling at the back of his mind. Perhaps it was that "surprise entertainment" planned for the evening, or just the miniature roses, he did not know. Either way he could not burst into her room, shake more information out of the already nervous, red-eyed Bessie, nor stay home all day. One of them had to make an appearance, so he ate a hurried breakfast before calling for the carriage. At the last minute Henrys pressed on him a heavy leather pouch from all the servants.

"Any horse in particular you would like me to put it on?" Carleton asked sarcastically.

"Oh, your Lordship will know which one," was his only reply.

It was late, and Carleton had a lot on his mind as he stepped out to the coach, so he only noted in passing that the second coachman was on the box. Must be Jeremy's day off, he reflected, before returning to wonder how he could explain to the Duke that his precious daughter-in-law was absent again. The three carriages from Berkeley Square were filled and ready outside, and Ferddie's just filed in behind, without any conversation, so no explanations were necessary yet. It was when they all reached their seats in a box at the finish line that Elizabeth's absence was noted. No one was terribly surprised after her nonappearance of the evening before, though they were all sympathetic that she, of all people, should miss the excitement. Margaret announced they would have to memorise every detail of the spectacle so dear Elizabeth might not be miserably disappointed. Spectacle it was, too, with all of London's nobility out in their finery, the ladies especially, in their spring gauzes and new bonnets, looking like fashion illustrations. Bands played, crowds milled about, paying more attention to each other than to the horses on the field. The Ardsley Cup was the third race, with no one giving much heed to the first two. Only when the trumpets blared and the horses were paraded for viewing did the spectators finally show some interest in the proceedings. The horses in the Cup race made a complete round, led by white ponies, and the Carleton box joyfully picked out Elizabeth's big chestnut. Bets were placed, including the servants' wages. Ferddie bet deeply, that confident. The Duke also placed a handsome sum with the stewards, joking that he would need his winnings to pay Elizabeth's stud fees if her horse won. Margaret was nearly bouncing in her seat, to her mother's displeased eye, by the time the horses were returned to the starting area, where their jockeys mounted up. Field glasses were trained across the oval, but the distance was too great to make out much detail. They could see the colours of the jockeys' silks easily, the green of the Marquis of Rockingham, the purple and white of the Earl of Oxford, whose horses were the heavy favourites despite the number of Elizabeth's friends. Bething's colors were yellow and white.

"Oh, poor, poor Elizabeth," Margaret moaned as there was some delay in mounting the Pride's rider.

"She must be really ill, I'm sure," said the Duchess, believing it to be so.

"She was very nervous about this evening," Carleton said, wanting to believe this instead.

"No, that ain't it at all," said Ferddie. They all turned to him expectantly, purposely not seeing the peculiarity of Milbrooke's answering for Carleton's wife. "She was upset about the jockey, mostly, besides being tired and excited. He'd hurt his wrist during a trial run or something, and her man was having trouble finding a replacement. Seems they'd raised the colt like a pet and it wouldn't take to strangers. See, they've settled it." All eyes turned to look where the handsome chestnut was mounted and turning toward the starting line. Carleton was staring at Ferddie, his mouth open in horror. He snatched up Margaret's glasses and fixed them on the yellow and white silks. Ferddie followed suit, more in curiosity at Carleton's behaviour than in comprehension. Then—

"Great God in Heaven!" he exclaimed. "Never say it's—oof!" An elbow landed in his midsection. A gun was fired and the horses were off in a blur of motion and colour. Margaret pulled her glasses back, while Ferddie simply lowered his, too dumbfounded to watch.

The Pride was far behind at the start, coming raggedly to the line. As the horses passed the finish line for the first time, the big chestnut was somewhere in the centre of the grouped field of horses, boxed in by older, more experienced horses—and jockeys. A horse directly in front of the Pride at the rail suddenly picked up speed to move on the leaders; the Pride followed right behind before an outside horse could nose him out. When the two were clear of the pack, the Pride moved away from the rail. The Duke groaned. Elizabeth's horse now had more distance to cover, with the two leaders, the favourites, pulling farther ahead as they passed the starting line again, heading for the finish. The chestnut was even as the second two horses passed that mark, and gaining. A nose ahead, a neck, then a length, two, and challenging the front runners!

"Outside! Take him outside again!" Ferddie was howling, recovered in the excitement. The crowd was going wild, too, and Margaret was shrieking in Carleton's ear. The second horse seemed to be tiring a little, dropping back, so the Pride passed him easily as the roaring grew and grew. At the last turn the Pride was still three lengths behind the strong leader. It did not look promising for the big chestnut. Then suddenly he put on a burst of speed, lengthening his stride as if he had just been out for a promenade before; now he would just show the crowd what racing was all about. The spectators were ecstatic at this display, pandemonium breaking out when the distance shortened... narrowed... closed. Folly's Pride passed the finish line, just in front of the Carleton box, a good head in front.

Carleton exhaled, not remembering having breathed during the race. He was being hugged and pummelled and shouted at in wild congratulations, as if he had had something to do with the win, while the real champion was making his victory lap around the track. The Pride was prancing like a circus pony, looking for all the world as though he knew the applause and thrown flowers were all for him. The jockey was waving happily to the screaming crowds. Then the circuit was complete and Robbie Jackson came to lead the Pride to the winner's circle, where a blanket of red roses was draped over the horse's neck. The officials were standing by with the trophy and the crowd hushed expectantly, but nothing was happening. Carleton only realised why when a steward hurried up to the box and Ferddie gave him a shove, while the Duke muttered "Fool" under his breath. He had been watching the jockey continue to pet the horse; now he went quickly down to the field to accept the congratulations of the officials. The Marquis also shook hands with Jackson before accepting the Ardsley Cup itself, a massive, two-handled silver monstrosity filled with more red roses. Under the eyes of hundreds of people, the officials, his family, happy bettors, he removed a rose from the trophy and solemnly handed it to the jockey. He looked up at a dirt-streaked face with enormous brown eyes, only one brown curl edging out of the yellow cap.

"It was a superb race," he said. "I know my wife would be proud." Then the crowd was cheering itself hoarse as Jackson led the Pride away. An official detained Carleton to tell him the prize money would be transferred immediately, the Cup fetched Monday for engraving. He also apologised to Carleton for any difficulties there may have been over entering the horse. By this time the Marquis was almost incoherent with the dread of anticipating that Elizabeth would be recognised, waiting for hoots of laughter or at least a thunderous bellow of rage from the Duke. The crowd's cheering subsided to a happy rumble, however, and the Duke was busily collecting his side-bet winnings from his cronies. Margaret wanted them all to leave immediately, to hurry home and tell Elizabeth. It was only Ferddie's quick thinking that avoided this new opportunity for disaster.

"Oh, I'm sure her groom's already sent a boy overland, ain't that right, Carleton? We could never catch him with the carriages. Anyhow, I'm certain Lady Carleton ain't expecting the whole party to walk in hours early. Besides, I've got money on the fifth race."

Carleton could only nod dumbly, thankfully. Didn't she know, hadn't she any idea what this could have meant? She would have been disgraced, ostracised from all Society. No one would have accepted her invitations, or offered any. God, it was *his* name she would have shamed. Relief was giving way to anger. He did not remember getting through the afternoon, only that Ferddie's hand shook slightly when he handed Carleton his winnings from the stewards. By the time Carleton was in his carriage on his way home, alone except for the ugly cup and the roses, he was in a towering rage.

At Grosvenor Square Carleton directed the coachman to drive directly to the stables. There, as he had expected, Jeremy was wiping down Juno, whistling happily while another man worked on Jupiter. They had even used his own horse! Of course, none other could keep up with the mare. Jeremy touched his cap when Carleton neared but hardly looked up from his work.

"Fine race, wasn't it, Jeremy?"

"Aye, my Lord, I was just tellin' 'Arry a—"

"You're fired."

"Yes, sir." Jeremy went back to rubbing and whistling.

Carleton stormed off, pausing only to take the trophy from the coachman. He went to the front door, hammering at it until it was opened by a startled Henrys, who stood aside just in time to avoid his master's rush down the hall and up the stairs. Carleton halted at the landing to put down the "damned silver flowerpot." He searched in his pockets, removed a large envelope and tossed it down the stairs. Bills and coins flew out at the butler's feet. Henrys never moved, only staring open-mouthed as Carleton rehoisted the cup and charged up to his wife's bedroom door. He kicked this one open, slammed the trophy down on the dresser and pointed glaringly to the door. Bessie dropped the hairbrush she was holding and ran out of the room, pulling the door shut behind her. Elizabeth pulled a robe to herself. She was clad only in a short chemise, just beginning to dress. Carleton took two steps farther into the room and yanked the robe out of her hands.

"What, modest, Lady Carleton? You, who could make a spectacle of yourself in front of an entire race meet? No, don't turn away!" He grabbed her shoulders to make her face him, shaking her in his anger. "You have offered me every imaginable insult, but I have tried to ignore it. You have turned my friends and my servants against me; you have carried on with the most notorious rake in London; you have behaved like a hoyden in the parks; and you have denied me my rights by marriage! I have stood it all, Elizabeth, but no more! This was too much today. If you are going to behave like an irresponsible child, without any care for your good name, then I shall treat you like one!" With that he raised one leg to her dressing stool, tossed her across his knee, and began smacking her bottom. "How dare you"—*whap!*—"make a laughing-stock"—*whap!*—"of yourself"—*whap!*—"with those damn horses!" *Whap!*

He released her and she fled to her dressing room door. When she realised he was not following her, she turned and glared back at him. Her eyes were filled with tears, but she would not cry until she had had her say:

"Lord Carleton, I could not make myself a laughing-stock with my horses; you have already done it with your . . . your fillies. Furthermore, my Lord, my bedroom door has never been locked to you except for one hour while I bathed, and afterward, by accident. You would not listen to me then; you had better listen to me now, for my door will not be locked in the future, either. Only from now on I shall sleep with a pistol by my bed. I dare you to enter my bedroom again!"

The dinner party was a great success. Everyone agreed that even if Elizabeth did not appear to be in perfect health, the excitement had restored her spirits. The Duke sat by her side at dinner, re-running the race for her, patting her hand in pride. Ferddie, on her other side, kept glancing at her nervously. Moving down the table, Margaret was enthusiastically debating a stable of her own with Hendricks and Rutley, and Sophie across from her. Lady Palmerson, neither impervious to his charm nor susceptible to his flattery, was enjoying *le Comte*'s dinner conversation cum-seduction. The Duchess was relieved to see her daughter-in-law looking so much better; maybe now that the pressure of the race was over Elizabeth and Alexander could reconcile whatever differences they had had. Carleton, at the opposite end of the long table, could hardly see his wife around the centrepiece—that damned Ardsley Cup, roses and all. He saw that she was sitting a little straighter than usual, though charming the Duke, as always, pretending that nothing had happened today beyond her horse's victory. He had to admire her poise and acknowledge her courage. He himself was too numb from the storms of the emotions he had gone through that day to do more than nod and smile at the ladies beside him. He was only now admitting to himself how deeply he had wronged Elizabeth, how monstrously he had behaved, especially on this, her night of triumph. He stood and lifted his glass in the first toast after dinner.

"On my engagement I toasted a horse; today the horse is honoured, yet I propose a toast to my wife. No one knows how much she had to sacrifice to make today's race possible, how much of her own spirit and bravery went into the running of it. Ladies and gentlemen, to my wife." It was no atonement, just all he could think of. Everyone stood and drank to Elizabeth's health. A moment of hush followed this solemnity, then the Duke stood and also saluted Elizabeth, "Whose heart, at least, was with us at the racetrack." Carleton almost choked. Ferddie jumped to his feet to drink to the horse, which was seconded many times, followed by toasts to the trainer, felicitations to Robert Carleton and Sophie Devenance, birthday congratulations to Wesley Northwell, cheers for Elizabeth and Carleton as hosts of a fine dinner. At last, all of the toasts having been made, the ladies prepared to withdraw. Carleton raised his hand.

"We have forgotten someone very important. My friends, to the jockey!" He was answered by "Here, here," "To the jockey," "Fine race," and a brilliant smile from Elizabeth.

When the gentlemen rejoined the ladies in the drawing room, it was to find the furniture pushed near to the piano, the other side cleared of rugs. When they had all found seats, Elizabeth stood by the piano to ask everyone's attention.

"I would like to thank you all very much for your kindness, and especially one very dear friend who has agreed to play for us tonight. My surprise, Lord Ferdinand Milbrooke."

Most of the company was mystified, never thinking of Ferddie as more than a good sport or a man of the Town. Carleton wondered how Elizabeth had ever managed this coup with Ferddie so shy about his music. The first piece was a brilliant Bach fugue, which finished to a standing ovation, and a schoolboy grin from Milbrooke. As pleased as punch, he announced he was going to play some waltzes; if anyone cared to dance, they should. He played as he had at Bething's Folly, with love and sensitivity. No one could fail to recognise his mastery, especially when they could compare his renditions with those of the indifferent orchestras at most dances. There was something about the piano solo waltz, in a small room, with beloved people... but no one rose. They were, of course, waiting for the hostess. Ferddie was oblivious; Elizabeth was growing disturbed. Carleton, who had been lost in the music and his memories of Ferddie's last "concert," suddenly recalled himself and rose to take his wife's hand. He began to speak as he led her to the other side of the room.

"This is for appearance sake only, my Lord," she threw back at him. "Save the chit-chat for your... your admirers."

"I deserve that, even if I have not many admirers here tonight. Please, Elizabeth—"

"I would rather listen to the music, my Lord."

"Couldn't we sit somewhere and talk during the next dance then?"

"No, sir, I do not feel at all like sitting this evening, thanks to you. And I really do not think we have much to say."

Margaret and Hendricks joined them on the floor, then Robert and Sophie, so there was no chance for further conversation. Elizabeth next danced with the Duke, Carleton with Duchess Claire, the Count with Lady Palmerson, and so on around the company, some dancing, some just enjoying the music. There was little idle chatter but a great deal of good will, in most of those present, at any rate. When Ferddie was done, apologising that he knew so few songs well enough to play, he was duly applauded and congratulated and punch was served—out of the Ardsley Cup. Elizabeth was teased unmercifully about her partiality for the gangly monstrosity, and Ferddie for hiding his talent so long. The Duchess was quick to notice how tired Elizabeth appeared to be growing, so she developed a convenient headache, at which the entire party started to dissolve.

155

The good-byes took a while, however, leaving Elizabeth obviously drained by the time Ferddie, the last guest, kissed her cheek.

"I've invited Milbrooke to have a glass with me in the study," Carleton told her, "but you go up. Shall I call for Bessie? No, well then, good night."

The Marquis and Ferddie settled in the comfortable chairs from the old bachelor rooms, loosening their neckcloths, propping their feet on the tables. Henrys poured out a decanter, poked at the fire and left.

"You know, Ferddie, you've been damned good to Elizabeth and me; a lot of help in these scrapes. No, I mean it. You must be pretty fond of her to have played tonight, besides."

"Of course I am, you know that. She's a fine girl—what are you getting at? If you are about to accuse me of romancing your wife, you are wasting your time, old boy. She wouldn't know how to be unfaithful, and I certainly wouldn't try to teach her."

"I know, Ferddie, though I once... No, what I'm getting at is that I think I shall be going away. Would you look after her? I... I intend to ask her if she wants a divorce."

"A divorce? Are you off your head? I'll look after her, of course, but she won't have me, you know, if that's what you're after. She really loves you, though Heaven alone knows why."

"I've treated her abominably, I know. It was a misunderstanding, but I have ruined it for good, now. I... I struck her."

Milbrooke was on his feet instantly. "God, Carleton, if I could call a man out over his own wife, I'd do it. If you have hurt one hair of that girl's head I'll—"

"I didn't hit her head. I'm sure I hurt her feelings more than her posterior, but I don't think she will ever forgive me."

"Well, you will never find out by sitting here. Damn,

what a day it's been. I'm off; about time I had an early night." He set his glass down and left Carleton behind, watching the fire for a while, wondering if he could ever forgive himself. After a while he went upstairs, taking a candle from the hall table and one of the Ardlsey Cup roses from the vase which now held them.

He scratched on Elizabeth's door and, receiving no answer, pushed it open. There was still no response so he walked over to the bed, shielding the candle with his hand so as not to disturb her. She looked so small in the bed, so fragile, this champion jockey. He smiled, even when he saw the pistol on the covers next to her hand. He set the candle down on the night table while he emptied the chambers of the small, pearl-handled weapon. Elizabeth still had not stirred, so he laid the weapon down, put the rose on top of it and said, "Miss Bethingame, I am truly sorry if I have hurt you"—words from another time. He bent to kiss her gently, tenderly—and was shocked by how warm her lips were. He felt her cheeks, her hands. Lord, she was burning with fever!

"Elizabeth? Elizabeth!"

# FIFTEEN

The doctor was disgusted to be summoned from his warm bed in the middle of the night to attend a typical case of what he called "debutante's disease."

"Why, anyone could just look at the lady and see she was exhausted. Too much gadding about, not enough rest. And not a proper diet, either, I'll wager. Her body just started protesting, that's all. Look at you, my Lord, you don't look much better. You're all a pack of fools, that's what," he grumbled on his way out. He did leave instructions for a tonic, nourishing broths and "Don't let her out of bed for three days. I'll be back tomorrow, in the daytime, thank you."

Carleton relayed the instructions to Mrs. Henrys, who was already busy in the kitchen. She sent him off with some cool lemonade, the best thing for fevers, she said. Bessie was not about to let the Marquis near her mistress, however, not even after he discharged her, with as much success as he had had with Jeremy.

"What, and leave you to tend her? You've done enough as is!" Carleton countered with Bessie's proven failure to look after Elizabeth properly, which only won him a "Ha! That's how well you know Miss Bitsy!"

They settled the squabble by dividing the remainder of the night, Bessie sitting up with Elizabeth first, bathing her forehead with damp cloths, offering her chilled drinks, while Carleton got what rest he could. He returned before dawn to relieve Bessie, who was too tired to argue more. Elizabeth was sleeping peacefully, much cooler to the touch. She stirred once, so he awkwardly lifted her to drink. She opened her eyes, but Carleton's presence confused her.

"Alexander? I won, didn't I? The Pride... we won?"

"Yes, darling, you won. Now go back to sleep." Her eyes were already shut when he lowered her to the pillows, a smile on her lips.

At ten o'clock Mrs. Henrys came with broth for Elizabeth, announcing she'd serve the mistress herself; his Lordship's breakfast was waiting downstairs, unless he wanted to be ill also. Then the Duchess arrived and insisted on sitting with her daughter-in-law until Bessie took over. Carleton got some rest, the doctor called again, Ferddie came by. Dozens of bouquets were delivered, to congratulate Elizabeth on her victory, then still more, wishing her a speedy recovery when news of her illness got around. The Duchess took some flowers home with her, before Carleton could throw them out. Carleton took dinner in Berkeley Square, assuring the Duke that Elizabeth was in no danger, that he and the Duchess might return to Carlyle the next day without anxiety. He promised to bring Elizabeth to the country as soon as the doctor said she could travel, for "a proper recovery."

Back at Grosvenor Square, Bessie told the Marquis that Elizabeth had eaten a good meal and was resting comfortably, with no signs of fever. Carleton refused the maid's wish to sleep on a truckle bed near Elizabeth, so again they took turns in the chair. Carleton had nothing to occupy him for his watch—his wife never moved, except to snuggle deeper in the pillows—but his thoughts. As dawn came, lightening the room, he found pen and paper and began composing a letter.

*Dear Elizabeth,* he wrote, *I am convinced that my presence here will keep you from the peaceful rest the doctor insists you have, so I am going away for a few days. You must not exert yourself! Ferddie will stop by frequently to see if you need anything, and I'll leave Jeremy, too. The Duke and Duchess have returned to Carlyle. They beg me to bring you to them when you feel able to travel. The Duchess carries messages to Lady Burke, who incidentally writes that Princess has had her foal—a colt—what a price you'll get for him! Mr. Sebastian has already received inquiries about the stables; he is keeping lists for you, of course. He has also received the transfer of your prize money—£10,000!*

*Elizabeth, I do not know if I have any right to your forgiveness, yet I humbly ask it. I have been so wrong, Elizabeth, I only pray it is not too late. If you can ever forgive me, I swear to make it up to you. I know I can make you happy if you allow me to try. If not I will get you a divorce somehow; or I'll go to Carlyle, where you need never see me again. I shall return at the end of the week, hoping to find a second chance waiting for me; but either way, I remain—Yrs., Carleton.*

*P.S. A groom arrived with a message from Jackson; he was starting home with the Pride and "she's here Friday." Those were Jackson's exact words, the groom swears, whatever it means. Please let Jeremy or Ferddie handle it. Or put it off till Saturday when I shall be here.*

*P.P.S. One thing I do not apologise for, darling. I still think you were shameless to ride in the Cup race, but I love you better for it.*

He folded the note to hand to Bessie, for delivery the next day. He gave his valet instructions to pass along, then went to sleep for a few hours. When he woke, he spoke to Bessie, ate and departed in the carriage. He had left explicit instructions with the servants and a message with Milbrooke. Only Henrys knew where he could be reached in case of emergency, which the doctor had assured him was highly unlikely.

Elizabeth received the note Monday night. A tear trickled down her cheek, proving she was still foolishly weak, she told herself.

By Tuesday morning she was thoroughly bored and healthy enough to demand real food. She badgered the doctor for permission to go downstairs, if she did not dress. Ferddie came by and played for her as she lay on the sofa.

Wednesday she came down for meals and began to bother Milbrooke to take her for a drive.

"Under no circumstances, Elizabeth; I gave my word to Carleton I'd keep you in the house till he returned, and I mean to do it, too. It won't do you any good to scowl at me, either, because for once I agree with him."

On Thursday Elizabeth dressed, sent notes round to her friends that she was much recovered, and tried to convince Ferddie again, to no avail. Friday morning saw her eating a hearty breakfast, then visiting Mr. Sebastian in his office. He reluctantly handed over the bank draft she wanted—it was her money, after all—but he absolutely refused to accompany her to Tattersall's that afternoon.

"A horse auction? I should say not! His Lordship gave definite instructions that—"

"Yes, I know." She sent for Jeremy next.

"I'm sorry, ma'am, truly I am. But 'is Lordship made me give my word. Said it was for your benefit; besides 'e'd 'ave my skin. Don't you go thinkin' as any of my boys'll take you, neither, 'cause they won't; so you just forget about it 'til 'is Lordship gets back."

"But I have to go, Jeremy, I just have to."

"Yes'm, but the horses is out getting new shoes anyway, 'is Lordship's instructions."

Her last hope, a slim one indeed, was the butler.

"Henrys, would you be so kind as to call me a carriage?"

"No, madam."

"I didn't think so."

Elizabeth went to her study to write a note to Ferddie; if he would not take her, perhaps he would at least go in her stead. She was walking up the hall to hand the letter to Henrys when she heard him at the door:

"I am sorry, *monsieur*, Lady Carleton is not accepting callers. I will convey your regards. Good day, *monsieur.*"

"Henrys, wait! *Monsieur le Comte*, how kind of you to come by! Would you by any chance be free this afternoon?"

A great many of Elizabeth's other acquaintances were also at Tattersall's that afternoon, unfortunately, for a great many tales were soon circulating about young Lady Carleton again, who was too sick for callers but could attend the horse auctions with a disreputable French nobleman. More interesting yet, she went home with Rutley and Northwell midway though the proceedings. No one knew if she had made any purchases, although it was not unusual for serious buyers to give bids to the auctioneers in private beforehand. In Elizabeth's case it was wise, for the interest of such a notable horsewoman could only improve a horse's credentials, and price. The Count, however, purchased a fine pair of showy greys which he was not at all reluctant to discuss, both that afternoon and evening in the clubs.

Ferddie was incensed when he'd heard of the escapade from Rutley. He drove immediately to Grosvenor Square, but Elizabeth was contrite. "Ferddie, I just had to go. I know I shouldn't have, I know Carleton will be furious again, but I had to. Please don't you be angry with me, too."

"Why did you have Northwell take you home? Did the Frenchman insult you?"

"No, not exactly. Ferddie, it was my own foolishness, truly. I will not see him again, I promise. I shall even go straight up to bed and not stir until Carleton gets home, so don't look so fierce, my dearest of good friends."

Milbrooke wasn't satisfied, nor pleased to hear Elizabeth's name mentioned everywhere he went. He located the Count at one of the clubs that evening and politely, ever so politely, mentioned that Lady Carleton would not henceforth find pleasure in *monsieur*'s company. Contented, he moved off to watch a card game.

Now the Count had not had a particularly satisfying day himself. He had miscalculated Lady Carleton badly, something he was not in the habit of doing. He had not only suffered a blow to his self-esteem but a financial setback also in those fancy dappled greys. They were certainly a handsome team, and very effective with his habitual black clothes, but costly. He had been counting on Elizabeth; now he would have to press Lady Palmerson a little harder. A shame, really, when Lady Carleton was so appealing in her own right, aside from the money and the chance to repay Carleton for the difficulties with Yvette. And now some young popinjay was warning him off....

The next acquaintance of the Count's to enter the club was treated to an enthusiastic description of de Rochefonte's new team, and their price.

"Come now, Giles, where'd you get that much blunt? I thought you didn't have a feather to fly with."

"Ah, but I have...friends," the Count said, much louder than necessary. The room quieted considerably in the hope of a new scrap for the gossip mills.

"Must be a good friend, indeed, to put up that kind of ready." His acquaintance laughed, knowing full well what kind of friend the Count had in mind. "Where was this friend last week when you had to borrow the price of a ticket to the opera?"

De Rochefonte looked around, making sure of his audience. "My friend only recently came into this money, a matter of luck, you might say, though I, of course, always took a great *pride* in our friendship." The Count's chuckle drowned in Milbrooke's thrown brandy.

"*Monsieur*," Milbrooke announced, "I find your choice of waistcoats in deplorable taste. Black is so depressing."

Carleton arrived home late that evening. Elizabeth was peacefully sleeping, the household at rest, so he decided to find Ferddie at the clubs or wherever he may be to tell him he was back. He never met up with his friend, although rumours about him were flying. At first Carleton could make no sense of it...the Count's waistcoats, pistols at dawn? There was a sick feeling in the bottom of his stomach as he probed deeper... Tattersall's, matched greys. Ferddie would never have challenged the Count over anything like that; the Count was known to be a much better shot. Then the dread was not nameless any more... Elizabeth, her prize money. He pieced the story together as best he could as he drove from club to party to his friend's rooms, thankful he'd kept his own coach with him. Time was running short, and no one could tell him where the duel was being held. Neither Northwell nor Rutley was home, so they were in on it, but where? In desperation Carleton ordered his coach back to Milbrooke's lodgings—not even Ferddie would undertake a duel without a night's sleep. It seemed he would. Carleton grabbed his friend's valet by the collar and lifted him in the air, preparatory to decorating the wall with him, when the man allowed he might have a guess as to the duel's location.

There was only one more detail the Marquis had to have and, thankfully, there was time for it. The coach raced for Grosvenor Square.

"Elizabeth... Elizabeth, wake up." He shook her shoulder gently.

"Carleton?" she asked, smiling sleepily, then when she saw his face: "What's wrong?"

"Listen to me, there is not much time. Did you go to Tattersall's with the Count?"

"Yes, but—"

"Elizabeth, what did you buy with your prize money?"

She sat up in bed, righteously pulling the sheets up to cover the flimsy nightdress she wore. "My Lord, I do not like your tone! If you wish to start that again, it is none of your affair. The money was mine according to—"

"Damnit, woman, Ferddie's life may be at stake! Did you pay for the Count's new greys?"

"No, of course not. I think he wanted me to, but why would I?"

"And you don't love him?"

"Love him?" she asked, incredulous. "I never want to see him again. He... he made some very unkind remarks."

"And do you love me, just a little?"

"I've always loved you, Alex, but what has this to do with Ferddie?"

"The Count is saying you paid for his horses, as a lover would. Ferddie called him out." He kissed her quickly on the cheek as he rose to leave. "I knew it was my fight, not Ferddie's; I just had to make sure you wouldn't mind if I won."

"Mind? My God, Alex, you could be killed! Don't do anything foolish!"

"No, darling." He smiled. "I think I have done enough foolish things for one lifetime."

As soon as Carleton was gone Elizabeth raced to her wardrobe, pulling a long hooded cloak over her nightdress. She stopped on her way out of the bedroom door, turning back to rummage in her night table for the pistol before running off down the back stairs and out to the stables.

She met Jeremy coming back inside from seeing what all the commotion was about, with his Lordship's carriage tearing up and down the road. He knew he was in trouble the minute he saw Elizabeth, all wrapped up, heading for Juno's stall.

"Jeremy, we've got to go after him. You know where he went, don't you?" When there was no answer, she went on: "The blacks can catch the coach, I know they can, if we hurry." Jeremy only shook his head, until she pulled the gun from under her cloak and levelled it at him. "You can tell Lord Carleton I threatened you. As a matter of fact, Jeremy, I am going, with you or without you; if you try to stop me I shall put a hole right through you."

He was already lifting the saddles down and tossing her harness parts.

Carleton was peering out of the carriage's window for any signs of activity in the misty half-light. What if he had come to the wrong place? No, there were horses beyond those trees.... He leaped from the carriage before it came to a stop, dashed across the open space. Ferddie was just lifting a pistol from the box Rutley held when Carleton reached them. The Marquis squared his broad shoulders, drew back his right arm and brought it up with every ounce of his considerable strength, hitting his best friend squarely on the chin. Ferddie went straight down and did not move. Northwell and another man, the doctor, most likely, bent over him. Rutley's mouth just hung open. Carleton bowed low to the Count.

"At your service, *monsieur.*"

A babble of voices broke out: "Highly irregular." "You can't do that, Carleton."

"But I have done it. I trust it meets with your approval, *monsieur?* After all, what satisfaction could you get from old Milbrooke, while just think of the implications if you put me away, *n'est-ce pas?* Of course, I am a better shot than Ferddie, so your chances are not so good; but it all balances out, does it not?"

The Count nodded, tersely accepting Carleton's challenge over his seconds' protests. The doctor was looking offended at the whole business. Ferddie still had not moved.

Carleton removed his topcoat and inspected the pistol Rutley now held out to him. He stepped out to the open space, his back to de Rochefonte's. It was curious, he thought while the seconds moved out of range. He really did not want to kill this man. He would gladly *delope*, fire into the air, if he had any thoughts the Count would follow suit. He could not chance it.

"Fourteen paces, turn and fire," someone said. "One ... two ..."

The Marquis was surprised at his mind's clarity. Everything had happened so fast. Had he told Elizabeth he loved her?

"Five ... six ..."

He could hear some noises intrude on the eerie stillness of the empty park, then two black horses loomed up from the shadows. It couldn't be, he told himself. Not even Elizabeth would—"Ten . . . " She was off her horse, bending over Ferddie, then out of his line of sight. "Twelve . . . " She shouldn't see—"Fourteen."

There were shouts. Carleton turned and brought his pistol up, aimed. Elizabeth was coming into the line of fire, her pistol gripped in both hands, facing the Count.

"No, Elizabeth, it's empty!"

The Count had turned, aimed, was startled by the commotion, fired. Elizabeth went down. Carleton steadied his own piece and fired. He dropped the gun without even looking at his opponent and ran to his wife. She was kneeling now, holding her arm. He tore her cloak off to look at the wound.

"Good God, Elizabeth!" The wound was merely a graze at the top of her shoulder, but she was practically naked! He pulled the cape around her again and lifted her in his arms, heading for the carriage. He nodded the doctor and Northwell over to the Count. Rutley ran ahead of the Marquis to open the carriage door, tossing Carleton's jacket in. Ferddie was standing up now, shaking his head, when Northwell called out, "He'll live, Carleton!"

"Ask him who paid for the damn greys," the Marquis called back. "Then tell him to get out of the country." As he reached the carriage with his burden, he noticed Jeremy mounted on Jupiter, struggling to hold the frightened mare. "Leave Juno for someone else to bring. You ride ahead for the doctor. And this time you are really dismissed," he shouted angrily at the groom's receding figure.

"That's all right, sir," came back through the mists, "I already works for 'er Ladyship."

The carriage started up the minute the door was shut on Carleton, Elizabeth still in his arms. Now he turned her cloak back and pressed his folded neckcloth to the wound, which was just barely trickling blood. He never said a word.

"Alex? Are you very angry?"

"If I don't warm your bottom over this, it's only

because I am a saint. Whatever made you do such an insane thing—or should I not ask?"

"I had to, Alex, to tell you about the horse! I never told you what I did spend my prize money on at Tattersall's, only what I didn't. It's the mare Robbie wrote about; we've been waiting and waiting for a horse from that line, and the money to buy her. She's perfect for the Pride, and for the Folly, to start a new line."

"You almost got yourself killed to tell me about your damned horse?"

"Oh, no, Alex. She's not my horse; she's yours, your wedding present. I—"

Whatever else she was going to say was forgotten in a very long, tender kiss.

The doctor was there waiting in Elizabeth's bedroom—at least they had waited for dawn for this nonsense—and Bessie with hot water, when Carleton carried her upstairs Henrys had a brandy poured for the Marquis as soon as he came back down. He was writing hurried messages when the doctor joined him, declining a glass.

"At this time of the morning? Bah. Next you'll be asking me to cure you of that! Well, you had better go on up to that wife of yours. She's already raising a fuss, wanting to get dressed and come down, or some such nonsense. More spirit than sense, I'd say, but she's in perfect health."

Carleton took the steps two at a time and opened Elizabeth's door without knocking. She was trying to put a dressing gown on while Bessie was angrily protesting. Carleton just stood by the door.

"She won't listen, Lord Carleton, and I know you're going to blame me..."

"Out, Bessie, out." He shut the door behind her, then slowly walked toward his wife. He untied the sash of her robe.

"But, Alex, I've got to see about Ferddie and—"

"Ferddie's coming to dinner." He gently lifted the robe

169

off her shoulders, letting it fall to her feet.

"But the doctor said I was perfect..."

Laughing blue eyes moved over her body, naked except for a small bandage, and one corner of his mouth twitched up. "I know."

A long time later Elizabeth stirred and sighed. "How sad that we wasted so much time, Alex."

He pulled her closer and began kissing her again, while his hand caressed her.

"You know what I wish?" she asked a minute or two later. "I wish you'd married me for love."

"You precious idiot, why else would I have?"